ANNE THROUGH TIME

ANNE THROUGH TIME

A Magical Bookshop Novel

HARMKE BUURSMA

Illusive Press

ISBN 978-1-962506-98-4 (ebook)
ISBN 978-1-962506-99-1 (hardcover dustjacket)
ISBN 978-1-962506-97-7 (paperback)

Edited by Megan Sanders
Author photo by Patterson Photography
Cover design by Getcovers.com

Published by Illusive Press
info@illusivepress.com
www.illusivepress.com

For more information about Harmke Buursma and her books visit
www.harmkebuursma.com

First Edition, 2023

Because everyone deserves a love story

Contents

"If it is true that there are as many minds as there are heads, then there are as many kinds of love as there are hearts."
-Leo Tolstoy, 1828-1910

I

The Letter

November 1814, Westbridge

"Give it to me. I want to read it." My little sister stood on her tiptoes, reaching for the letter I clutched above my head. The tips of her fingers still fell short about a hands-breadth despite only being a few years younger than me. Regardless, I made sure to keep my hand elevated while she swatted my arm.

"It isn't addressed to you," I told her.

She pouted, brows knitting together as she focused on the piece of correspondence.

"Mary, leave Anne alone," our mama chastised from her favored spot on the settee. "Must you always quarrel? It is as if I've raised a pack of wolves." Mama sighed and shook her head, flicking a chestnut curl behind her ear. "Anne can read it to us when your father returns."

Mary hesitated, her eyes still peering at the letter. "But Mama—"

"Mary..." Mama cut in, her voice curt. Her lips pursed as her gaze swept over us. "I was under the impression that I had raised good obedient daughters, or should I return you both to the wilderness? No?"

Mary lowered her slippered feet to the floor and turned towards Mama, nodding once, disappointment etched on her face.

I couldn't help but smirk. My younger sister was easily excitable and could be quite persistent when she wanted something. Of course, I was just as interested in the contents of the letter; our brother only wrote to us once a month. Mama often commented that Randolph did not write home enough. During dinner, she would lament between bites of food that her son had nearly forgotten her. But, ever since Randolph left for university, it had become a tradition to read his letters while we gathered together in the sitting room.

Mary, determined not to give up, spoke once more, "Perhaps we can read it again when Papa returns?"

"Your father will be home soon. How do you think he would feel if we had ignored his existence and read Randolph's letter without him?" Mama patted the space beside her. "Now, come take a seat."

Mary glanced back at me, scowl deepening when she caught the smirk on my face. I stuck out my tongue, chuckling when Mary primed herself to have another go at me. I stepped backward and kept my arm raised.

"Anne, you too... Stop teasing your sister."

"Yes, Mama." Chastised, I straightened my face, lowered

my hand, and laid the letter down on the side table while Mary slinked off to the fireplace. With a huff, she sank beside Sergeant, our dog. A pair of bleary eyes opened, and the old bloodhound lifted its giant head, transferring it to Mary's lap. A trail of slobber glistened on the plum fabric of her dress. Mary scratched the hound behind its long, fawn-colored ears.

"Careful not to soil your dress, Mary." Mama reached for a leaflet on local happenings. "Soot is such a challenge to remove, not to mention all of Sergeant's saliva." She flipped through the pages as I sat next to her and crossed my legs. Despite her warning, a soft smile still appeared on Mama's face.

I was watching the flames dance in the fireplace when the front door slammed close. Sergeant lifted his head and let out a howl, another long trail of saliva dribbling from his jowls onto the stone floor.

"I'll take those, sir," I heard Elsie, our maid, say from the hallway.

Mary rose and brushed off her dress, smiling from ear to ear. "Papa." Her face brightened as she hurtled herself towards the man entering through the doorway.

"There are my girls." He patted Mary's head and freed himself from her grasp. "Elsie's just taken my string of pheasants. I dare say I shot the most fowl today out of every man present. We shall be having supper fit for a king."

"That is wonderful," I told my father.

Mary pulled Papa's sleeve. "There's a letter from Randolph. Can we read it?"

Papa looked down amiably, but he seemed tired, his appearance a bit worn around the edges, the skin beneath his eyes darker than usual. However, that was to be expected since Papa had been up before dawn. I doubted that I would ever understand why men liked hunting. There had to be more to it than standing in fields and shooting at birds.

Mama tutted. "Mary, give your father some time to rest. He has been out all morning."

Papa flashed his wife a smile. "No need to be concerned on my behalf, darling. I am fine. Let us find out what news Randolph has to share with us." He loosened the cream-colored cravat around his neck and moved to the round chair beside Mama. "Now, who shall do the honors? Anne?" His eyes rested on me.

I nodded and grabbed the letter from the side table.

Then Papa turned to Mary. "And will you fetch me my pipe?"

Mary handed Papa the delicate clay pipe and squeezed in between Mama and me. I sliced open the envelope with a silver letter opener from the side table while Papa packed his pipe with tobacco from the lead tobacco box with its pretty lid decorated with grape vines.

Unfolding the letter, I smiled at Randolph's handwriting, unsightly slashes that had never improved despite Mama's constant admonishments when he used to practice his penmanship.

Papa let out a puff of spiced, earthy smoke while Mary pressed into my side to make sure she could read along with me.

I cleared my throat.

To Mr. and Mrs. Blakeley

Dear Papa and Mama,

Dear Mary, if you are reading this by yourself, I advise you to wait until our parents and your sister are there to read my letter together with you. Dear Anne, thank you for keeping your sister in line.

I have missed you all while I've been away at Oxford, though I have some exciting news to share; this year, I shall manage to return home for Christmas. It pleases me to take a break from academia to celebrate the Yuletide with my family.

And yes, in case you were wondering, Mary, I shall return with gifts. Baxter, one of my classmates, knows all the best places in Oxford to purchase presents. He has been showing me places around the city that I had never noticed before.

Mary squeaked next to me. "Randolph's coming home and bringing presents." She nudged my arm. "Go on, does he say when he will be here?"

I snorted and continued reading.

Once this letter has been sent, I shall arrange to finish some last-minute assignments and secure travel. You can expect me home in a week.

On another note, my class is preparing for next semester to start abroad. An excellent art program in Greece will host us starting the new year. I've already pledged my attendance for the coming year; I will merely require a banknote to be sent to the headmaster to settle the funds. I can share more in-depth particulars when I've arrived home.

Your loving son and brother,
Randolph Blakeley

Mama's eyes lit up. "We'll need to notify Mrs. Grantley that Randolph's room needs airing out."

Papa grasped Mama's hand and squeezed it. "There's plenty

of time before our son returns. I am certain that our house-keeper can wait to be notified until later today."

"Of course, you are right, darling." Mama leaned back against the seat.

Mary was rereading Randolph's letter in silence. I handed her the paper so she could hold it herself while I processed Randolph's words.

Greece. Randolph was going to Greece. I felt a stab of envy souring my joy at seeing my brother again soon. Randolph was studying and going abroad, all things I wanted but was unlikely to ever accomplish.

Mama was obsessed with making my debut in society this spring, and my persuasions to postpone it for another year fell on deaf ears.

Perhaps Randolph could use an assistant to carry his inks and brushes, and I could travel along to Greece. I knew it was a flight of fancy, but the thought made me smile nonetheless.

Papa wheezed and let out another puff of smoke before sucking on the end of his clay pipe. Sergeant whined from his spot in front of the fireplace. The wood had almost all been consumed; only a few flames flickered around the remaining bits and pieces. Papa rested his pipe on the table and stood.

"I can call Elsie over," Mama said. But Papa waved her away.

"No need to call the maid." He lowered himself to one knee next to the dog and patted its rump before grabbing two logs from the firewood bin and placing them in the center of the fireplace.

I turned to Mama. "What should we get Randolph for Christmas? Perhaps a better luggage set since he will be traveling?"

"Or a new summer wardrobe." Mary tapped a finger against her cheek in thought. "It is hot in Greece, isn't it?"

Mama smiled. "Those are both splendid ideas. We should —Robert?"

Mama screamed as Papa's eyes turned wide, and half of his face drooped downwards like the drips of paint on a canvas. He crumpled forward, his body landing on the ground with a loud thud. "Robert?" she said again, voice wavering and laced with fear.

I jumped up from the settee and hurried to Papa's side. My knees skidded across the stone floors as I sank to the floor. "Papa?" I touched his back, but he did not stir. I turned to Mama. "Help me turn Papa.

Mama stared unflinchingly, unable to grasp what was happening. "We should call for a doctor." Her voice turned as thin as gauze.

With all my strength, I managed to roll Papa over. I felt for his heartbeat but detected nothing. What could I do? Was there anything I could do? I did not know medicine. I shook his shoulders. "Papa, please wake up."

"We should call for a doctor." Mama's hand trembled as she stood. "Robert, a doctor is coming."

I felt numb. I wanted, no, needed space, but my first concern was Mary. She was still sitting in the chair, fat tears rolling down her ashen face.

I let go of Papa and motioned toward my sister. She hugged me tightly when I got to my feet. I kept her face buried in my dress so she would no longer be able to see Papa.

Elsie ran to us but stopped at the doorway, her eyes widening at the sight of Papa.

"Send out word that we need a doctor," I told the maid. She nodded grimly and turned on her heel. Panic surged through my veins, but I knew that composure was necessary to guide my family through this difficult time.

I turned to my mother, her face etched with sorrow and concern. Her eyes mirrored my pain, yet I saw a glimmer of uncertainty flickering within them. She spoke softly, her voice quivering with a mix of fear and desperation. "Anne, my dear, what if there's still something we can do? Shouldn't we stay here by his side?"

My heart ached at her words, for I, too, wished for some miraculous intervention that could bring my father back to us. But deep down, I knew that his passing was final and that we could do nothing to change that. Gathering my strength, I reached out and took my mother's hand in mine.

"Mama," I whispered, my voice trembling with emotion, "I understand your worry and your desire to stay by his side, but we must trust in the help that is on its way. Elsie has gone to fetch assistance, and it won't be long before someone arrives to guide us through this."

Tears welled up in my eyes as I continued, my voice trembling. "We must be strong, Mama. Father would want us to gather our composure and await the help that is coming. There will be time for us to mourn, to grieve, and to find solace together. But for now, we must retreat to the parlor and let others handle what we cannot."

My mother looked into my eyes, her expression a mix of pain and understanding. She nodded, her grip on my hand tightening. "You're right, my dear Anne." Her voice filled with a quiet determination. "We must trust in the help that is on its way and gather our strength for what lies ahead. Our family will face this together, as we always have."

***

Papa was laid out in the parlor, hands folded neatly on his chest and his combed dark hair a stark difference against the cream-colored casket lining. It was strange to look at him; he appeared peaceful, but whatever part it was that made my father feel like himself was missing. I felt detached as I gazed at him; I had the strangest sensation of looking upon a stranger. Nevertheless, my heart ached.

It had been a few days since his passing—apoplexy, according to our physician Dr. Marlowe. Mama had barely left his side since. She had always been thin, but these days she appeared to shrink in on herself, verging on emaciated. I wrapped my arms around her, hugging her tight before exiting the parlor, the bones in her rib cage prominent beneath my fingertips. She remained passive, sitting stiffly on a chair she'd pulled up next to the casket.

It happened so fast. One moment we were all together, discussing Randolph's latest letter from Oxford, then Papa keeled over. There was nothing any one of us could have done, Dr. Marlowe had told us. Still, I could not keep from wondering what would have happened if I knew what I was doing or if I had been faster. What if there had been signs that we'd missed? Papa had complained about a persistent headache.

I sighed as I crossed the hallway. Our housekeeper, Mrs. Grantley, had arranged for Elsie to take some simple crepe dresses from our closets and dye them black. No fashionable colors during mourning. Mama, the few times she left

Papa's side, walked around with her hat covered in black lace, obscuring her face. Her figure was like a wraith haunting the upper circle at the theater on Drury Lane.

Going up a flight of stairs, I finally found Randolph in Papa's study. He'd only arrived that morning. He looked worn out, his face drawn as he sat wide-legged in Papa's chair, peering over stacks of papers and leather-bound ledgers. He wore his regular attire except for his cravat, which he had switched out for a black one.

My arrival jolted him from his musings. He looked up at me as I placed my hand on his shoulder, offering him a bit of comfort. "Brother, come take a break downstairs. I can have Elsie brew us a pot of tea."

Randolph yawned and raked a hand through his hair, mussing up his dark curls. "I can't. There's much to go through. Father..." He stopped himself, frowned, and shook his head. "Never mind, I just need more time to sort through all of this." He motioned at the stacks of papers and ledgers.

I squeezed his shoulder. "You've only just arrived. Surely settling his estate can wait until after Papa's been—" I paused. None of the words that flashed through my mind sounded right. I pursed my lips, stepping away from Randolph and towards the mess on the desk. "The papers will still be here tomorrow and the day after and the day after that. Come downstairs with me. You have not spoken a word to us, and Mary has been so excited about you staying with us for the holidays." I leaned forward and tugged on his sleeve. "Of course, now..."

"Yes." Randolph nodded. He cleared his throat and laid

down his pen. "I'll join you, but only briefly; I do have to continue going through these files."

"Fine." I grasped his now empty hand and smiled at him. "I am glad to see you, brother. We've all missed having you around."

Randolph's eyes softened. "I've missed you too, sister."

2

Dignity And Honor

The next day we buried Papa in the town's cemetery. Westbridge's vicar, Mr. Willoughby, and most of our neighbors showed up to give their respects to Mama. John and Beth Easton, the Brocklehursts, and many more familiar faces attended, dressed in their finest dark-colored clothing.

Mary clung to my arm, crying. I supported her and swallowed back my tears; my throat ached with the strain. Randolph was quietly watching the vicar say his piece about Papa. The creases between his brows deepened. He had not slept much. As soon as he'd finished his cup of tea yesterday, he had returned to the study, nose pressed into the papers. He hadn't left until late in the evening; I hadn't been able to sleep either, so I'd heard him shuffle past my room.

I watched Randolph and wondered if there was something else. Perhaps he regretted coming home from Oxford. At least he knew he was going to leave again in a couple of weeks.

Randolph flinched as the vicar ended his speech. I did not have time to ask if he was all right before the first townsfolk lined up and headed toward us.

Beth and John Easton paid their respects, moving from Mama to Mary, then me and Randolph.

Beth squeezed my hands, her cheeks reddened by the wind. "I am so sorry for your loss. If you or your family need anything, we are always available." She flashed a watery smile. "Mrs. Avery, our cook, has made some of her apple tarts, and I've taken the liberty to send a basket to your home." Beth glanced to her side, noticing the line of people waiting behind her. Her eyes widened. "Well, I won't keep you. My condolences, Anne."

"Thank you."

Beth nodded and moved on to Randolph.

When we returned home, the air inside was heavy with grief, our hearts burdened by the weight of my father's passing. The somber atmosphere was interrupted by the sound of the doorbell announcing the arrival of yet another neighbor's servant offering condolences and assistance.

As Mama and I stood in the foyer, surrounded by the fragrant lilies and sympathetic murmurs, I could sense her growing unease. The neighbors were kind-hearted, their gestures genuine, yet Mama's pride was a fortress she held tightly onto, shielding us from the vulnerability of accepting help.

I opened the front door. Mrs. Patterson, a long-time acquaintance, approached us with a basket filled with comforting foods. "Anne, dear, I hope this brings you some solace in these trying times." Her eyes were filled with empathy. Unlike most households that sent a servant, Mrs. Patterson had decided to stop by herself. I felt touched by the effort. Mama, however, felt otherwise.

Mama forced a strained smile, her voice tinged with formality. "Thank you, Mrs. Patterson, for your kind thoughts. But truly, we have enough to sustain ourselves. We cannot accept charity."

Mary, always the curious and compassionate one, spoke up, her voice gentle but persistent. "But Mama, why must we refuse the help of our neighbors? They only wish to lend a hand in our time of need."

Mama waved Mary away with a stern glance and returned her attention to Mrs. Patterson. "We appreciate the gesture. Still—"

"It isn't charity." Mrs. Patterson shook her head, taken aback by Mama's reaction.

"We cannot. I hope you understand. Good day, Mrs. Patterson." Mama ushered her back out of our foyer and closed the door in front of her perplexed face.

Mary blanched, her bottom lip shaking as her eyes were on the verge of crying. "Mama..."

Mama sighed, her expression serious and unsmiling. "My dear, we must maintain our dignity and honor your father's memory. We cannot rely on others for our sustenance. We must rely on ourselves and our own family."

"But Mama," I interjected, my voice pleading, "these acts of kindness are not meant to diminish Papa's memory. They are gestures of love and support from those who care about us."

Before Mama had a chance to retort, another visitor arrived: the Eastons' servant, holding a platter of apple tarts, a gift from my friend Beth. I felt a flicker of hope. "Mama, please." I clasped my hands together. "It's a gift from Beth. The Eastons have always been generous to us. Can't we accept it?"

Mama's eyes bore into mine, her disapproval evident. She opened her mouth to decline once again, but I interrupted her, my voice filled with urgency. "Please, Mama. We've always received gifts from the Eastons. It's a token of their friendship, and it would mean so much to Beth if we accepted it."

Reluctantly, my mother sighed, her resolve wavering. "Very well, Anne. If it means that much to you and Beth, we shall accept it this time."

A glimmer of relief washed over me as I accepted the tarts from the servant and carefully placed them on the table in the foyer. It felt like a small victory, a triumph over my mother's pride.

As the servant departed, I turned to resume our conversation, only to find a burly and serious-looking man with deep-set brows standing at the door. His presence was unexpected, and his unfamiliar face stirred a sense of unease within me.

The man contorted his mouth into a smile, nodding at me. "Can I speak with the man of the house?"

Mama's stern voice rang out behind me. "My apologies, Sir. We have just returned from my husband's funeral. If there is nothing else that can be done, we should like to return to the comfort of our home to mourn in peace."

Curiosity filled me, and I couldn't help but ask, "Why do you ask about the man of the house?"

Before an answer could be given, Randolph descended the stairs. He approached the man, seizing him by the arm, and led him outside, instructing him to wait. As the front door closed, shutting off their conversation from our ears, I exchanged a puzzled look with Mary, my younger sister.

"What do you think that was about?" I whispered to her, my curiosity piqued.

Randolph returned after a few minutes, his countenance glum and troubled. I approached him, eager for answers. "Randolph, what did that man want?"

He brushed off my question, his tone dismissive. "It was nothing, Anne. Just a misunderstanding. Don't concern yourself with it."

But I could sense there was more to it, a secret he was unwilling to share. The tension in the air lingered, leaving me with a sense of unease and unanswered questions.

3

And Still We Must

A loud noise woke me from my dreams. Moonlight shone in through the window, setting the room aglow in soft gold. I sat up in bed and swiped at my face, brushing my hair away from my forehead, when I heard another sound like something hard hitting the floor. Wondering what was happening downstairs, I stood and covered myself in a robe.

I tiptoed past the upstairs corridor, careful not to awaken my sister or Mama, then trudged down the stairs to find Randolph cursing at the hat stand while rubbing his right shin. The front door was still open behind him.

I shushed my brother and gave him a stern glance. "What are you doing coming home at this hour?"

"You sound just like Mama." Randolph's face reddened, and he turned away from me before hurrying to bend over and pick up the hat stand. His movements were slow and uncoordinated, but he managed to maneuver the stand back into its usual spot beside the front door.

A sharp blast of wind fluttered my robes and chilled my skin. I shivered and pulled my robe tighter around myself, closing the gap at my clavicle.

"Randolph, can you please close the door?"

My brother straightened himself and stared at me before grabbing the brass handle and pulling the door closed behind him. The stench of liquor followed him around.

I stepped down to the hallway floor, observing my brother's behavior. Something felt off about him. On the rare occasions I had seen my brother drink, he would turn jovial and talkative, chatting everyone's ears off. This evening Randolph looked...sad? I could write it off to our Papa's passing, but somehow, I had the sense there was more to it.

"Brother, I've never seen you like this; you seem different. Is something the matter?" I grabbed his sleeve so he would stop turning away and so I could look at him.

His eyes met mine for a moment when he retorted, "You haven't seen me in a long time, sister. Perhaps I've changed." Randolph pulled his arm from my grasp. "You should return upstairs. It is late."

"Brother, I know something is the matter. Why can't you tell me?" My voice came out in a tone that reminded me of Mama whenever she scolded us. "Is it Papa, or did something happen at Oxford? You were as normal as could be expected when you returned home."

"It is of no matter to you."

"What isn't? You can share things with me."

Randolph sighed and stumbled past me. "I need another drink."

"Another one?" I raised my brow, but he'd already turned away and faced the sitting room, his hand against the hallway wall for purchase. "I think you have had enough for one evening," I called out after him. "What would Papa and Mama say if they saw you return home drunk?"

Randolph snorted and glanced back at me, his expression odd. "What would Papa say, indeed." He let out a round of short staccato laughs without much mirth behind them; the sound pierced my heart like buckshot. "I suppose we shall never find out now, will we?"

I was dumbstruck by his response and hesitated as he ambled into the sitting room. Then I picked myself up and followed him.

"What do you mean? This is our Papa you are speaking about. How could you—How could you be so insolent?"

Randolph, with a singular focus, moved to the bar cart in the corner of the sitting room, decanted a bottle of scotch, and poured himself two fingers of amber liquid into one of the crystal glasses. He did not bother lighting a candle or doing anything else besides drink.

I crossed my arms and glared at Randolph as he lifted his glass and tipped the contents back. "Have you not had enough?"

Randolph shot me a glance and grabbed another glass, filling it with the same liquor, then held it out to me. "Trust me, if you knew...you'd like another as well."

"If I knew what?" I grabbed the glass, watching the swirling liquid before turning my gaze to my brother.

He poured himself another drink.

I frowned. "If I knew what?" I returned my drink to the bar cart and tried to lift Randolph's glass from his hand, but he evaded me. My stomach churned as my mind wondered what could be so difficult that it drove Randolph to drink. "What are you not telling me?"

Randolph avoided my gaze "Anne...." His voice was soft and pleading.

My hackles raised when he said my name. "Don't Anne me and stop avoiding the question. Tell me the truth."

Randolph stepped back and emptied his glass again. His brows furrowed when he turned to face me, his breath reeking of alcohol.

"We have no money."

I watched my brother's face, waiting for the rest of his confession, but he'd quieted. None of it made any sense.

"What do you mean we have no money?" I held my breath, willing him to explain.

Randolph raked his hand through his shaggy hair and sighed. "I did not want to burden you with this, but it is true. We are nearly cleaned out and still owe a debt to a collector in Bath."

I felt lightheaded and had to steady myself against the bar cart. My arm trembled when I asked, "Surely, you must be mistaken?" It could not be true. Mama and Papa had never mentioned anything about our finances. I shook my head. "There has to be an explanation. Perhaps the debt collector is wrong? You could go there and speak to him, sort everything out."

Randolph's hand tightened around his glass, his eyes

softening with what I could only assume was pity. My brother pursed his lips. "If only that were true...if only it were a mistake, then, perhaps—" Randolph slammed his glass down on the bar cart and cursed in exasperation. I watched him as he paced the sitting room, his face red.

"When I returned home, I wanted to make sure all our finances were in order and every outstanding bill had been paid. I poured over the ledgers and receipts that Papa had left and found out that the entire fortune had been squandered. Even Mama's bridal price and the money set aside for you and Mary are gone. All gone. Everything gambled away."

"How can it be? I've never noticed a change. Everything here has continued as usual."

Randolph let out another mirthless laugh. "You would not have noticed. Papa has been keeping his gambling a secret, taking out loans to keep up appearances whenever necessary. After settling his debts, there will be hardly anything left to live on. We may need to sell the house. Perhaps even get sent to debtors' prison."

The news unsettled me. My throat thickened, and my chest squeezed. My eyes burned with the effort of holding back the tears forming behind them. They would not help me now.

"This is our Papa. I cannot believe he is capable of this."

"And yet, he was," Randolph scoffed. "A few hours after I mailed my letter home, the headmaster reached out to me about the outstanding payment for next year's tuition. I was supposed to head to Greece with my class. I thought there had been a mix-up and it would be resolved when I received news that Papa had passed away." Randolph stopped pacing and sat down in one of the club chairs, leaning his head in his palms. His body was obscured in the shadows of the dusky room. "I wish Papa had told us," he muttered. Then, even softer, he added, "Why didn't he tell me?"

"I-I don't know." I stuttered over my words. I did not know what to do or how to comfort my brother. My mind still had to fathom the idea that our father had been a completely different person from the man that had raised us. I thought that I knew who Papa was, but apparently, I had been very wrong.

I crossed the room and sat in a chair beside my brother.

Randolph lifted his head and glanced at me, his mouth a thin line. "Anne, I'm going to meet with the debt collector and ask for a payment plan to help give us some more time to find an answer. However—"

"What if you can't?" I cut in. "Then what happens to Mama and Mary and...us?"

Randolph chewed his lip. "We would need to sell the house. It and our belongings are the only things of value that we own. Before that happens, I could try and find work, though that would not earn us enough to stay here indefinitely. The best-case scenario would be if you..." Randolph stopped, his lashes lowered, red cheeks deepening in color.

I gritted my teeth. "You can finish the sentence." I stared at him, willing him to acknowledge the truth that I had already understood. "The best-case scenario would be if I married someone wealthy."

Randolph nodded. I could tell that he felt ashamed to even mention it. "Mary is too young, and Mama is only recently widowed. I do not see another option."

"Right." I wanted to close my eyes and scream. Only a week

ago, I was dreaming and hoping to travel outside Westbridge and discover my purpose in life.

I suppose I had found my purpose; becoming a wife, saving my family from ruin.

"Anne, we do not need to be hasty. I will venture to Bath and speak with the debt collector about a payment plan. Perhaps there will be other solutions in the future."

"Perhaps." I shot my brother a lukewarm smile to soothe his worry, but I knew that life had changed for me. All I could do now was to ensure that Mary was none the wiser. I wanted my sister to be able to still have the life she wanted, no matter what that might look like. "Will you tell Mama and Mary?"

"We should." Randolph straightened, stretching his spine against the back of the chair. "Mama and Mary need to know that we cannot keep spending like usual. We cannot afford any more trips to the modiste or lavish dinner parties. "

"It would break Mama's heart to learn about the finances," I protested. "You've seen how she has been since Papa's passing."

Randolph sighed again, furrowing his brows. "And still we must."

4

A Sponsored Season

Spring 1817

I found myself in a spacious and comfortable room with soft bedding and thick drapes that blocked the outside sun. I could hardly believe it would be my bedroom for the coming weeks as I joined the London Season with Beth Easton.

My suitcases had been brought up by a maid that belonged to the rented home near Covent Garden. I lifted one onto the bedspread and opened the latch. My eyes were drawn to the ribbon on top of a stack of folded dresses and shifts. My sister, Mary, must have sneaked it into the suitcase, something to remember her by while I was away from Westbridge. The thought brought a smile to my face.

I heard a knock on the bedroom door, followed by Beth entering my room.

She grinned widely, taking a long glance around the space. "What do you think of your room?"

Beth picked the room across from mine that looked out across the front road. There would be plenty of foot traffic and carriages riding by. Mine was more peaceful, overlooking the back garden and stables of the rental property. But then again, I preferred the quiet, while Beth had always thrived on being at the center of excitement. I had found her earlier, staring out of the window, longing for the events to come.

I picked up Mary's navy ribbon and laid it gently onto the vanity before turning to Beth. "The room is wonderful. I cannot thank you and your brother enough for sponsoring my season."

My cheeks reddened when I addressed Beth. Without the kindness of Beth and her brother, John, I would not have been able to afford to go to London. I would not be able to find an eligible bachelor to marry.

These past few years had proved how difficult it was to find a suitor when one no longer had a dowry to their name—even with my brother vouching for me and persuading eligible men, there had been no takers. If I could not find someone to marry me and save my family from ruin this season, then I feared it might never happen.

Beth bounced through the room with boundless energy and seated herself next to my suitcase. She picked at a few of my dresses. "We shall go to the modiste tomorrow. Then you can find a new wardrobe as well."

I was grateful to Beth, John, and his wife, Rose, but I felt ashamed when I thought about how I had treated John and Rose not too long ago. In my desperation to save my family from financial ruin, I had tried my hardest to snare John into being my husband, especially when Rose showed up out of nowhere. It was clear that John was taken with her even then.

"There's no need," I told Beth. "I brought my dresses from the previous year. They will do."

Beth lifted her right brow. "Anne, you cannot possibly think that I will let you chaperon me at events without a new wardrobe..." Her smile widened as she held out her hand. "I mean to have fun this year, and I want to share that fun with you."

I grabbed her hand and let her pull me next to her.

"Just promise me that you will not report everything to my brother." Beth squeezed my palm. "For once, I would like to enjoy a bit of freedom without my brother's interference."

I snorted. "I will do my best. However, I really cannot accept this much. Everything you and your brother have done for me already... I cannot possibly repay it."

Beth shook her head. "We would never ask you to. You are my friend, Anne."

"Even after everything I said last year? How can Rose not hate me?" I sighed and leaned forward to rest my chin in my hands. I had lied and schemed, treated Rose like mud stuck beneath my shoes, all in my pursuit of John when I had not even loved him. My sole motivation was my family, and when trying to find an eligible bachelor, John, at the time, had been one of the top choices; he was wealthy, had a good family, and I was already friends with Beth. John also had none of the vices many other men dealt with, like gambling, drinking, or unkind demeanors.

"Anne..." Beth's voice turned delicate. My cheeks reddened

some more. "We are all aware of your... situation. Rose understands. None of us blame you for your past behavior."

I was uncertain of how to respond. I paused and muttered a soft, "Thank you."

Beth cheered up again. "Well then, let us get some rest and prepare ourselves for the modiste."

***

Beth and I both found some new fabrics at the modiste the next day. Despite feeling bashful about taking even more help from the Eastons, I was excited about receiving new dresses to wear. It would be nice to attend balls and dances in new outfits, although I wished I could have sent something new to Mary so she could have worn a new dress at home.

The trip to the modiste was not uneventful. Beth and Beth's maid, Estelle, and I followed a shop-girl past velvet curtains into the fitting room. We were not the only customers because a stout woman was already there sitting on an ottoman as she tutted a young woman.

The woman appeared to be around the same age as Beth and myself, with wavy red hair fastened into a bun at the top of her scalp. I wondered what it would look like undone; she did not seem the type to be confined by pins and clips, even if the swathe of fabric currently enveloping her was covered in them.

The red-haired woman stared at the stout middle-aged woman that I assumed was her chaperon with a wooden expression while a shopgirl was adjusting the fabric around her shoulders. One of the pins must have poked her because she let out a shrill yelp. The shop girl's face ashened while another worker hurried and adjusted the pins near the red-headed woman's bust.

"I apologize, miss. Let me change those for you."

The red-haired woman swatted the shop girl's hand away, scowling. "I do not like being poked and prodded like a pig for slaughter. Could you please take those pins and that fabric away?"

My lips quirked at her exclamation. I glanced over to Beth, who mirrored my amused expression. A giggle escaped my throat which I did my best to muffle with a well-placed cough.

The modiste, Ms. Taylor, entered the fitting room, ignoring the commotion, and with a fixed smile, turned to Beth. She told us she would fetch some more fabrics and left as quickly as she had entered.

With a whiny quality to her voice, the redheaded woman spoke to her chaperone, "Are we almost finished?" Her face darkened as the shop girl held a variety of fabrics up to her face. "I do not want or need a new dress." Her gaze moved between the middle-aged chaperon and the shop girl.

The chaperone tutted again. "Ms. Willa, your father has given me clear instructions to see to it you are fitted with a new wardrobe and accompanying accessories. You must make a good impression."

The shop girl hesitated beside the redheaded woman, unsure of what to do with the fabrics in her hands. But the chaperon waved her arm and urged the girl to continue while the redheaded woman glared. The shop girl held up a deep green silk next to the woman's face, its color drawing out the rich red hue of her hair. The woman named Willa remained unmoving, forcing her chaperone to get up from the ottoman.

Sounding aggrieved, the chaperon snatched the fabric from the shop girl's hand and spoke to the woman. "Ms. Willa, can you not be pleased to receive a new dress? Think of your father and how proud he would be to see you in it."

Willa snorted. "Proud enough to get rid of me."

I glanced at Beth again, raising my brows. We had barely been acknowledged by the two women, and now we were privy to this delicate conversation. Though she looked morti-fied at the moment, I knew Beth was going to recount every word of it after.

The chaperon was laying out lace trims across Willa's shoulder, trying to match it to the fabric.

Finally, not being able to keep quiet, Beth chirped out, "That color suits you."

I wanted to slap my face; I did not think that that was what the redheaded woman wanted to hear, but Beth was kind and liked complimenting other people.

Willa assessed Beth, her green eyes drifting to me for a mere moment. "Thank you." Then she turned to the shop girl. "You can take that one away; I need something unflattering, orange perhaps."

The shop girl's mouth dropped open, and I laughed in shock. Next to me, Beth stifled a giggle. The redheaded woman certainly was unexpected; you never knew what was coming next. Willa flashed me a bright smile before smirking at her chaperone.

The chaperone rolled her eyes and sighed. "What am I supposed to say to your father?"

"Tell him I have received a new wardrobe just as he wanted."

Willa faced Beth and me, explaining herself even though we were only strangers. "Father is pressuring me to join the marriage mart this year, but I have no intention of marrying anyone."

She said it so decidedly; I envied her confidence and determination. I wished I was in her position, having the choice and willpower to do what I wanted.

"Is this your first year?" Beth asked. "My brother did not want me to go, but I finally got him to agree." Then Beth pointed at me, and a wave of embarrassment rolled over me. "Anne has attended the London Season a few times."

Willa's cat-like eyes observed me before she nodded to Beth. "It is my first year... but my father is dead-set on getting me engaged and out of his hair."

"Willa." The chaperone gasped.

Willa rolled her eyes and scoffed. "Yes, I know. He is doing it for my own good, blah, blah, blah."

The chaperon pursed her lips after hissing, "We are in the company of others."

Willa shrugged. "We are all ladies here." She stepped towards us and extended her hand. "My name is Willa."

Beth greeted her first then Willa moved to me. I grasped her hand and introduced myself, looking up into her eyes.

Willa smiled. "Perhaps we will run into each other at one ball or another."

I found myself hoping that might be the case. Willa was sure to liven up any event. It would be a pleasant surprise if our paths were to cross again.

Willa glanced back towards the curtains where the shop girl entered with an ugly orangish-brown colored fabric that looked like something that had been moldering in someone's basement for a decade or more.

A grin appeared on Willa's face, much to the discontent of her chaperone. "Perfect. That will do nicely. Let us return home." The chaperone sighed while Willa shrugged pleasantly. "I am tired of being poked and prodded." Before leaving, Willa turned back towards Beth and me. "It was nice to meet you both."

After Willa left, Beth and I had the fitting room to ourselves so we could get measured and pick out the finished touches for our chosen fabrics. The whole process went by without a hitch; I had to admit that I kind of missed Willa's entertaining conversation.

5

Mandarins

Lady Westham's ball was our first event of the season. I wore one of my new dresses, a deep blue gown that Beth swore complimented my pale skin and chestnut hair. Beth's maid, Estelle, had wound my hair up into a twist, leaving small curls to frame my forehead. I gingerly touched the back of my neck while Beth led us through the crowded ballroom.

Drinks first. My mouth felt parched, and I needed something to lubricate my throat. Everything hinged on these events. There were a finite amount of balls and dances where I could attract suitors; I needed to make a good impression. My stomach was tied into knots at the thought of failure.

Beth was blissfully unaware of my inner turmoil as she stopped at the nearest table of refreshments. She had been smiling since before we arrived, excited about her first steps into society, something her brother had been very much against for the longest time.

I picked up two glasses of lemonade and handed Beth one, then I glanced around the room, observing the dancers swirling around the floor and the men walking the perimeter.

"Which one do you think will approach us first?" Beth asked.

I bit my lip and shrugged. Both our dance cards were still empty for now; we just had to wait for one of the eligible men to step forward and ask us to dance. Beth's eyes were trained on a foppish man wearing a blue brocade vest who was conversing with another, a broad-shoulder fellow with a smirk as bright as his polished top boots.

My stomach knotted as I waited by the refreshments table. Thankfully, the introductions with Lady Westham went by smoothly. Beth took care of that when Lady Westham's attention was drawn to me. Once we were acknowledged by the lady of the house, the two men Beth had been eying stalked over to add their names to our dance cards.

I was just about to say something to Beth when my eyes caught a glint of red, and a woman ran past us. The woman bumped her hip into a second refreshment table, scattering mandarins all across the floor.

I frowned as I caught sight of the woman's pained face. Her face was familiar, but I had not expected our paths to cross this soon. Beth shot forward to help the woman pick up the mandarins before I had a chance to react.

"Willa?" I muttered though Beth had already confirmed her identity.

Willa glanced at me, flashing a swift smile before she rubbed her hip and continued picking up the fruit, pocketing one into a slit in her skirt.

Willa addressed Beth's question. "Yes. You were there for my fitting." She returned the remaining mandarins to the table and glanced around, face flushing, when she noticed the number of guests staring at her and whispering behind raised fans. I could hear snickering coming from behind us. Her face squinted, and she looked embarrassed. "I apologize; I do not have time to speak. I have got to go." Willa dropped the last fruit on the table and ran towards a hallway in the back.

People were still whispering around us, and I worried that our association with Willa might hinder our chances to meet and dance with the men present.

"Wait," Beth called out after Willa.

I was concerned about Willa as well, but I had a duty to my family, and I had promised John Easton that I would chaperon Beth to the best of my abilities. Beth turned away from me, and I could tell she wanted to follow Willa.

I grasped her wrist. "Let her go. We have quadrilles to dance. I am certain Willa will be fine." This was one of the biggest events of the season, and we had to make a good impression. I could not let whatever was going on with Willa interrupt my goals. "That woman is an odd one."

Regardless, my eyes still flitted to the hallway Willa had disappeared into. No, I could not follow her and check up on her. The men from earlier were near; this might be one of the few chances I got to find a marriageable man.

Beth had no such worries, however. She looked between me and the hallway. "You can go ahead. I will only be a moment."

"Beth..." I wanted to chide her and keep her near, but I understood why she wanted to go. Willa had looked out of sorts. I had no other argument to make, so I simply said, "I am supposed to chaperon you."

Beth tilted her head. "I know, I will not be long. I just want to make certain she is all right. Enjoy the dance for me, please."

I wanted to chuckle; this was so like Beth, befriending strangers, taking in strays. I lifted my brow and smirked. "Fine, but if you do not hurry, I will dance twice with both men."

Beth laughed and leaned into me. "Scandalous, Ms. Blakeley."

I shook my head and let go of her wrist, watching Beth flit across the ballroom and into the hallway. Then I remained by myself, awkwardly standing beside the refreshment table.

I was glad when the man with the polished top boots returned for his dance, so I did not need to remain a wallflower for long. His palms were a bit sweaty as he gripped my hand and led me onto the dance floor.

"What is your name?" he asked as we formed a circle with other couples.

I lowered my lashes. "Ms. Anne Blakeley."

"And Ms. Blakeley..." he flashed me a toothy smile. "Where are you staying?"

The first notes of the music started, so I moved my feet into position for the country dance. "I am a guest of Mr. and Mrs. Easton. They are letting a home near Covent Garden."

The man nodded while we took turns stepping to each other's side along with the music. Instead of going left, he moved right and stepped on top of my slippered foot. I winced, but the man continued, oblivious to my pain. "That is a popular location."

I forced a smile on my face though his dancing did not improve. Though I wanted to make a good impression, I felt immense relief when the dance ended, and I noticed Beth signaling me from the sideline. I excused myself swiftly and hurried to Beth's side, though my feet were tender now.

"You may need to find a way to avoid him if your feet are precious to you," I lifted my poor mangled feet off the floor. My slippers now appeared quite worn; I might need another pair before long.

Beth grinned. "I saw. You were lucky to come away unscathed."

I glanced at Willa, who was standing beside Beth, tapping her finger against Beth's shoulder in a way that was supposed to be subtle. There was still an air of concern around her. Beth noticed the tapping and turned serious as well. I wondered what the two had been discussing without me.

Beth cleared her throat. "Anne...This is Willa Balfour."

I wanted to quirk my brow. Did Beth forget I was there when we met at the modiste, not even mentioning when we spoke to her only minutes ago? "Yes. We have met." I nodded to Willa and fanned myself. "It seems you are feeling better."

Beth hesitated, but Willa stepped towards me, a serious expression on her face. I stared into her cat-like eyes as she inched closer to me and lowered her voice to the softest whisper. "I am in a bit of a predicament, and Beth has agreed to help me. She will pretend to be me this evening."

My throat hitched at the sound of her voice, the husky quality at odds with her words. Soft notes of jasmine and honeysuckle clung to Willa's skin. What had she said? My mouth opened and closed. She wanted Beth to switch identities with her. Willa continued her explanation that Beth was supposed to take her place and meet an Irish duke.

"I wish I did not need to ask, but would you be willing to help keep up the ruse?" Willa blurted out before I could gather my wits. Cool skin brushed my palm as she grasped my hands. "I would be ever so grateful."

Beth was stifling a smile beside her; I wanted to give her a pointed look.

"Will you?" Willa urged again. She dropped one of my hands and grazed my arm. My gaze returned to her; I noticed the worry line between her brows.

I sighed and nodded though I did scowl a bit. "This does not mean that I agree."

"Thank you."

I shrugged and shook my head at Beth. "You are telling me everything when we are back in our rooms." What would Beth's brother think of me if he found out I let Beth switch identities? I was supposed to chaperon her and keep her safe. "I asked you not to get me in trouble. What would John say?" I just hoped she would listen to me and not push the limits.

Beth shrugged, a hint of defiance tinting her voice. "My brother is not here at the moment, and there is no reason for him to find out."

"I will take responsibility if it comes to that," Willa interrupted. "Please, do not worry." She placed her hand on my arm once more. I dropped my scowl and acquiesced.

6

Refreshments

Beth straightened, her chin tipping up as she glanced across the crowd. I followed her gaze to a man I had not seen before speaking with Lady Westham.

"Is that the duke?" I asked Willa.

Willa hesitated, her expression uncertain. "I suppose so."

"Have you never met?"

"No, how else would we be able to pull off switching identities?" Now that Willa spelled it out, I regretted asking such an obvious question. For some reason, whenever Willa was near, I became a bit muddle-headed. I looked at Beth, whose cheeks had turned pink as she took in the duke. The man was the same as most other men present, so I did not understand why she had such a strong reaction.

When Beth managed to pull her gaze away from the duke, she asked Willa, "Are you certain you want to go through with this?"

Willa rolled her eyes. "Yes, I am certain. A handsome face is not enough to make me reconsider."

Beth laughed and shook her head. "I cannot even pretend to understand you."

Willa shrugged, not sparing the duke a second glance. I would need to keep an eye on Beth, however, because she could not keep from staring at the man, though she quickly averted her eyes when he pointed toward us.

Willa pinched Beth. "Ready yourself." Her eyes assessed my friend, taking in her flustered state. "Remember... Willa Balfour, the daughter of the Marquis of Bambreich."

"The marquis. Yes." Beth's throat bobbed.

Willa pursed her lips, hesitating. "All right. Pretend to have an interesting conversation." Her green cat-like eyes locked with mine. "You, too. Let out a giggle or something."

I raised my brow, wanting to laugh at Willa's serious instructions.

"Let out a giggle or something. Pretend to be having an amusing conversation," she continued.

"I need to act now too? Next, I will receive a position on Drury Lane," I jested before faking a giggle. Willa improvised a story as the duke stalked toward us. I had to nudge Beth to pull her from her nervous stupor.

"And so, Father took us on an outing to the circus. Have you been? Oh, la, it was marvelous. Such a unique experience." I wanted to scratch my head at Willa's acting abilities. Perhaps *she* would have a future as an actress on Drury Lane. Even her voice had changed to a high-pitched coquettish tone, very different from her usual huskier sound.

Beth let out an airy giggle just as the duke arrived and

said, "Pardon me. May I introduce myself? I am Edmund Humphries, the Duke of Cashel." He lifted his right hand to his heart and bent forward. I, along with Beth and Willa, curtsied and lowered my gaze with enough deference fitting his station.

"Well met, your grace," Beth said once the duke had straightened.

He flashed her a smile. "Our host of the evening told me I could find Ms. Balfour among the three of you." He paused, waiting for one of us to respond.

"I am Ms. Balfour." Beth stepped forward, then nodded at Willa and me. "And these are my friends, Ms. Blakeley and... Ms. Easton." She stumbled a bit at the last part.

Willa must have caught the pause because she cut in. "How do you find London?" Beth straightened herself and then bumped her arm into me, casually pointing at something to her side. I glanced over to see what she was pointing at. I nodded when I saw it was the man in the blue brocade vest that had requested a dance.

Beth turned to the duke. "Would you care to dance, your grace?" She flashed a smile. Asking first was not proper etiquette, but I knew she was trying to get the duke to the dance floor before the other man reached our group; he might inadvertently spoil Willa's scheme. While Beth followed the duke to the dance floor, I grasped Willa's hand and turned to intercept the man in the blue brocade vest.

"I apologize," I told him. "My friend has already promised this dance to another. Perhaps another time?" The man frowned, but I waved him off with the help of Willa. Looking displeased, he finally turned and stalked off, presumably to ask another woman to dance.

"Good riddance." Willa's eyes flashed mischievously. "How about we venture back to the refreshments? We can keep a watch on Beth from there."

I chewed my lip, staring into her bright green eyes. "All right."

Willa hooked her arm with mine and pushed her way past the mingling guests until she reached the drinks and promptly pressed a glass of lemonade into my hands. I sipped from the glass while she snatched one of the mandarins and busied herself peeling the fruit. Beth stared at us from across the room. Willa smiled wide and waved when she caught Beth's stare.

"Do you genuinely think this is the smartest play?" I asked, moving in to stand beside Willa. From this angle, I had a clear view of the ballroom. I turned my face towards Willa, catching another whiff of honeysuckle. "Will the duke not figure out that he is seeing the wrong person? How are you planning to deceive your father?"

Willa's gaze met mine. "Those are a lot of questions... I must admit that I have not thought that far ahead. I hope that the duke will lose interest and the season passes without any other interference. My papa tends not to focus on the details as long as I do not flaunt my scheme in front of him."

"I see." I considered Willa's words. The social implications could be monumental if Beth was found out; however, if she managed to uphold the lie and the duke lost interest, then there would be no harm to her reputation.

Beth could be stubborn when it came to something she

wanted. If I tried to persuade her to drop this scheme, she might dig in her heels even more. My eyes flitted to where she was dancing with the duke, finding her gone.

I perked up, glancing around the room. "Beth and the duke are missing."

Willa looked around as well. "Perhaps they went outside?"

I raised my brows. "She was supposed to stay here so we could keep an eye on her."

"I highly doubt your friend is going to disappear into the night with my duke," Willa joked.

I blew out a frustrated sigh. "I suppose..."

"So you admit it." Willa's face brightened, and with some help from the candlelight glow from the wall sconces, I could count the freckles on her face.

"Admit what?" I shot out when I felt my cheeks heat. What was this feeling?

"That you are being overprotective of Beth." Willa's eyes sparkled as she teased me.

"I will concede that I am a bit... strict. But I promised her brother, and I owe him and his wife a lot of gratitude."

This quieted Willa. Her perpetual smile dampened a bit. I wondered what I had said that had made an impact on her.

Willa frowned a little. "Beth mentioned something earlier when I was in the hall. She said it was important for you to find a suitor."

"She did?"

Willa nodded and adjusted her bodice.

"Did she tell you why?" It wasn't like my family situation was some great secret, but I would have liked it not to come up straight away. Frankly, I felt a bit embarrassed, especially when Willa was so outspoken and forthright.

"She has not. And you do not have to either, that is, if you do not want to."

Willa appeared earnest enough. "Thank you... perhaps another time?" My voice came out a bit more hesitant than I was expecting.

"Of course. I am certain the three of us shall become better acquainted in time."

Willa perked up beside me, and I returned my gaze to the ballroom. Finally, I saw Beth winding her way through the crowd. I shot her a glare for good measure. When she neared, I closed the gap. "Where were you?"

Beth winced apologetically. She gingerly touched her hand to her lips, which appeared redder than usual.

"What did he do?" If the duke had kissed Beth and someone saw...

Beth glanced around the room and then grabbed my hand. "He did not do anything. I-I will tell you everything when we are alone."

"What happened?" Willa asked, linking her arm with mine and Beth's. Her voice quieted when she spotted the duke entering the ballroom. "Wait, we should leave the ball first."

I locked eyes with Willa and nodded, then the three of us wound our way past the perimeter of the room until we reached the main exit.

Lady Westham blocked our path as she spoke to a flamboyantly dressed couple. Willa unlinked her arm from me and interrupted our host.

"Lady Westham, I want to thank you for your gracious invitation to your ball. It has truly been a splendid evening."

Without too much chit-chatting, we were able to pass her by before the duke caught sight of us.

Willa pulled Beth into a hug once we exited the front door. "Thank you for playing along."

"You are welcome. However, I cannot understand why you would not want to meet him. He was..." Beth paused, red creeping up her face. "Perfectly splendid."

Beth's reaction worried me. From just one meeting, she already found herself infatuated with the duke. I was glad the charade was finished because I could not see a happy ending if it was not.

Beside me, Willa's tone turned teasing. "Indeed? Is that why the two of you were away for so long?" I watched Beth avoid Willa's gaze. "That is what I thought," Willa continued, chuckling. "Never mind. I am not interested in... that."

I shuffled side to side, my skin cooling as we stood outside in the night air. I wanted to call over a carriage and return to our Covent Garden home. "Is that it then? Are we finished with the charade? I, for one, am freezing and would like to return to my room."

Willa's lips lifted into a smile, and she deftly plucked a mandarin from the pocket in her dress. "I suppose so. I only agreed to the one meeting at the dance, and that has been fulfilled." Her long, slender fingers picked at the peel, stripping away layer after layer until the fruit was bare. She picked out a juicy segment and plopped it between her full lips. "But promise me," she said between bites, "that you will let me take you both out as a thank you." Willa grabbed another segment and extended it toward me. My fingers brushed hers as I accepted the piece of fruit. Willa's cat-like gaze made my heart skip a beat.

Beth, unaware of the strange feelings coursing through me, grasped Willa's free hand and squeezed it. "Of course, this evening has turned us into friends. You cannot be rid of us now."

Friends indeed, I thought as I savored the segment of mandarin. I was glad that the scheme with the duke was finished, and I had to admit that I felt excited at the fact that I would see Willa again.

7

Bambreich Manor

The next day, I found myself once again in the presence of Willa Balfour. Beth and I had ventured to her home, Bambreich Manor, after we had received a letter. I had made myself comfortable in a velvet chair in her sitting room while Willa paced the floor. Her beautiful red hair hung in loose curls along her back.

"What was so urgent? Is it something to do with the duke?" Beth asked Willa as she stood with her back towards the doorway.

Willa tiptoed towards the open door and ascertained whether the hallway was empty, then she shushed Beth. "Not just yet."

Beth glanced behind her with a puzzled expression. "Wha—"

"Hello, Papa," Willa cut in when a middle-aged man

appeared seemingly out of nowhere. She smiled widely at her father.

I tried to detect a resemblance between the two, but besides both seeming to favor a cheerful countenance and both being tall, I could detect nothing. Her father looked distinguished with a full head of dark hair and graying sideburns. He was wiry, whereas Willa had soft feminine curves that begged to be touched.

"Let me introduce you to my friends, Ms. Blakeley and Ms. Easton."

Mr. Balfour smiled genially. "It is always wonderful to meet any of my daughter's friends. Where did you three meet?"

"At the modiste," I said, clasping my hands in front of me.

"The modiste, eh?" The Marquis of Bambreich snorted. "Perhaps I need to beseech the two of you to change my daughter's mind about wearing new dresses." Willa's father's eyes twinkled with mirth.

"I have dresses aplenty, Papa," Willa said flatly, angling her body in a way to dissuade her father from entering further.

"I hope you do not mean the orange monstrosity you wore the other night." Willa faltered while her father lifted his chin knowingly. "That is what I thought." He sighed. "Sweetheart, please do your father one favor. You look so much like your late mother. I would like nothing more than to see you dress in one of her favorite colors."

Willa averted her eyes, her lips narrowing into a thin line. "I shall consider it."

"That's all I ask." Willa's father nodded and scraped his throat before turning to me and Beth with a smile. "Well, I shall return to my study and leave you girls to your own devices. Perhaps I will meet you both later if you stay long enough for a cream tea."

"I shall make sure they will," Willa assured her father. Then she waited until her father left to close the double doors.

The interaction must have taken a lot out of her because she leaned her back against the wood, her chest rising slowly with her breaths before she plastered on a smile again and glanced at us. I wondered what she was thinking, why she had looked so vulnerable for a moment. There was more to Willa Balfour than met the eye.

I wanted to put Willa at ease, so I reached out, placing my hand against her arm. "Your father is sweet."

Willa shrugged, still tense, before turning her ear towards the door again. Her father had already left, but she was still checking to be certain. "My Papa is," she said once she assured herself that we were alone. "However, I feel like he is pushing me away. Perhaps I remind him too much of my mother."

My heart ached for Willa. I was well aware of what the loss of a parent did to a family; my mother still had not recovered.

My voice softened as I gazed into her eyes. "She must have been very special. I am sorry for your loss."

Willa sighed and flashed a weary smile that did not reach her eyes. "Thank you. It..." she paused. "It has been a few years, but Papa is still in mourning. He has hardly left the house since she died, so I worry about him."

I nodded, wishing to reach out and hold her hand, but I did not want to overstep. "My father passed away two years ago. My mother has not even set foot in his study yet. It is still exactly as he left it, cluttered with his things." What I did not mention was that my mother still visited his grave daily and how she could not bear to see my father's study since it reminded her of all the secrets he had kept from her and us.

Willa stepped away from the double doors and walked around the room, fidgeting with her hands. "I think my father is trying to arrange a marriage for me to ascertain that I will not be left alone." Willa's face darkened as if a deep sadness enveloped her. "I do not know why he feels the need to arrange that. He is not going anywhere, and I like my life as it is." She chuckled sadly before Beth or I could respond. "Let us change the subject. We do not need to speak about my father. I invited you for a reason, after all."

"Yes," Beth said. "I was wondering about that. Does it have to do with last night?"

I perked up my ears. I had thought that the scheme with the duke had ended, but Willa had invited us here for a reason, and I doubted that it was for a mere social call, especially considering how on edge she was.

"It does," Willa said, confirming my suspicion. "And I apologize for shushing you earlier. I did not want my papa to overhear."

I disliked the drawn-out suspense, so I cut in. "What is it?"

Willa's eyes flashed to me before returning to Beth. "It appears the duke enjoyed his evening with you, Beth." She wiggled her brow.

I wanted to groan. Of course, he had; Beth had clearly been kissed by him.

"Uhm, he should not have?" Beth said innocently. I was pretty sure that I mirrored Willa's stony expression.

"Since he is under the impression that you are me and

I have no intention of getting married... no. It would have been better if he had disliked his interaction with you." Willa threw up her hands. "But what is done is done. However, I received a letter stating that he is coming to visit me and my father here tomorrow."

Oh no. That was certainly a predicament.

Willa snorted as she continued. "And my father cannot find out about our arrangement."

"What do you propose we should do?" Beth said, sitting down in one of the chairs as she finally grasped the severity of the situation.

"I have not thought that far ahead."

I was racking my brain for a solution. "Is your father aware that the duke is coming here?"

"No, I managed to sneak it out of the pile of letters."

"What if you managed to get him out of the house," Beth offered. "Keep your father busy somewhere? I could take your place in this room?"

I gritted my teeth. Willa's scheme was getting more and more complicated. Beth and I were supposed to focus on meeting suitors, not plot dalliances with a duke. "Willa, can you not send the duke a note and cancel?"

Willa considered, humming a soft tone. "What if he does not accept my cancellation and still turns up? He could take it upon himself to visit my father and me regardless."

I considered the risks. What if anything went wrong and Beth was exposed? What if John found out and made me leave London early? I could not return to Westbridge without an engagement.

Folding my arms, I stared at Beth and Willa. "It is a risky plan; anything could go wrong. What about the staff?"

"Let me fret about that." Willa continued pacing around the room. "I might be able to send them along with Papa. Perhaps leave one scullery maid to serve tea."

Willa might say that I should not fret about the details, but I was still worried. What if the staff gossiped? "What if the scullery maid tells anyone? And how do you plan to lure your father out of the house?" I shook my head. "I do not think this plan is going to work."

Beth frowned, seeming a bit deflated. "Is it not easier to stop our ruse now?" She crossed her legs. "We cannot keep this ruse going. What if the duke wants more visits?"

Willa lurched towards Beth and clasped her hands. "Please, Beth. I cannot do this without you. Will you please help me do this? I assure you I will keep my promise."

I felt annoyed at Willa's mention of a promise. Beth had confessed to me last night that she helped Willa in exchange for Willa's help in finding me a good match. And while I needed to marry, the idea of Willa helping me felt wrong somehow.

"Is that the promise that you will find me a good match?"

Willa bobbed her head. "Yes, I will make sure."

Her earnest answer only provoked my annoyance further. She did not care that if I found a match, I would marry. But then another thought crossed my mind; why was I even considering her opinion towards me?

Regardless, I did not want her help. I placed my hand on my hip. "I thank you, but I do not need assistance with finding a husband."

Willa's chipper smile faltered when she caught the tension in my voice. I raised my chin further, trying my hardest to remain calm and aloof.

"All right," Willa said, her eyes observing me. I could sense some interest in them that had not been there before. "Perhaps we can continue our friendship sans matchmaking. If that is amenable to you?"

A small flutter stirred my heart, and a smile slipped past my defenses. "Perhaps," I conceded. Willa and I gazed at each other until Beth's interruption broke the spell.

"So, what happens if I accept?"

Willa's eyes broke away from me, and she started listing things off on her fingers. "Step one, I will need to find a way to lure my papa away from the house. Step two, you need to be here, ready to pretend to be me. Step three, you need to dissuade the duke from wanting any future visits. Preferably you get him to revoke his intentions of marriage."

"Because that sounds easy enough..." Beth said. The sarcasm in her voice was layered on thick.

Willa stopped pacing. "His letter stated that he would be here around eleven. Will you be able to arrive before then?"

"I believe so."

We continued our planning when Willa's butler arrived and called Beth away to meet a visitor. The brown-haired guest introduced herself briefly before being pulled away by Beth. The situation was curious, but I supposed I would find out later how the woman had found Beth at Bambreich Manor and why.

I turned to Willa. "While Beth is dealing with the duke, what will you do?"

Willa's gaze turned to the side as she thought. I watched the expressions she was making as she mulled things over. "I would like you to come as well," she said.

"You would?" I was a bit surprised. I did not feel like I was bringing anything of value to the situation. Beth was indispensable because of her introduction to the duke, but I was merely Beth's friend and was not a necessary part of Willa's scheme.

Willa nodded. Her lashes lowered as she glanced away. "There is a circus in town which would be the perfect excuse to get my father and staff away from the manor. Perhaps you could go with me?"

My breath hitched. "I-I would like that."

Willa smiled. "I am glad." Then she looked to where Beth and the other visitor had strode off to. "They have been gone awhile. I should go check in on Beth."

Not much later, Willa returned with Beth and the other guest in tow.

"Melinda," the middle-aged woman reminded me.

"Beth has explained our situation to Melinda," Willa said. "She is here to help us."

I looked at the brown-haired woman. She seemed familiar somehow, but I could not quite place her.

Beth chewed her lip. Her eyes flashed to Melinda before she asked, "Can they... Can I tell them?"

Melinda gazed at Willa and me. "I reckon they will find out before long."

Find out what? I wondered. Willa's look of puzzlement matched mine.

Melinda strode towards the settee and pointed at the seat. "Can I take a seat?"

"Of course." Willa extended her hand.

"I might as well start with the most important fact," Melinda said as she fluffed the pillow and took a seat. She plopped down and made herself comfortable, spreading out her maroon dress and leaning her arm on the rest. "I am a time traveler."

"I apologize, what?" Willa went slack-jawed.

I had many questions myself. What did Melinda mean? "How do you know Beth?"

"I met Beth and her brother when I sent Rose to West-bridge."

Rose? John's new wife? Time travel sounded far-fetched, but Rose had appeared out of nowhere. I had frequently scratched my head at her accent and behavior. If she was from another time, it would explain some things.

But Rose had not been the only stranger arriving suddenly. "Then... Mr. Miller?" I looked to Beth for confirmation. My friend nodded. "Melinda also took William Chambers and Austin Miller to the future."

"So they are not traveling?" I would need some time to wrap my head around it. Compared to time travel, my problems were rather mundane.

"No. William chose to be with Austin in the future."

"Ah," I said. I did not know how else to respond. However, I did wonder why Melinda returned now.

"Are you here for Beth?" I asked Melinda. "Are you taking her somewhere?"

"I don't know this time," she said. "All I know is that I

am supposed to be here. I suppose I will find out eventually. In the meantime, I plan to assist you all with your duke situation."

8

Astley's Amphitheater

Despite Beth having the riskier task of entertaining the duke, I was nervous and fidgeting with my fingers, picking at a loose piece of skin near my fingernail.

"I will be fine," Beth assured me once the carriage halted near Bambreich Manor. "Try and enjoy yourself at the circus. I know how you can get..." She cocked her head as if urging me to disagree.

I let out a soft laugh. "I will try, but Beth... try and end things today. If you can."

Swiping her hands along her updo, she nodded. "Yes, today will be the final meeting with the duke. Then we shall return to our events." She seemed almost reluctant to say the words, though when she met my gaze head-on, she slipped an assuring smile on her face.

"All right." I watched my friend closely. I was worried that she had become infatuated with the duke, even after one meeting, but I hoped she would keep her wits about her. This scheme was one big distraction that both she and I could ill afford.

Beth smiled at me and opened the carriage door. The two of us exited onto the sidewalk where Melinda was already waiting.

Convincing Willa's father to go to the circus had been easier than expected during cream tea. Willa had acted surprised and almost a bit taken aback at how smooth her suggestion had gone, especially once Melinda twittered to Willa's father how she would love to go see the elephants.

"Ready?" I asked Beth. She was staring at the gated property. Beth needed to sneak around back where Willa was going to let her in through the servants' entrance.

Beth's face scrunched up into the sheer image of determination. I patted her arm. "Good luck." Melinda waved Beth off as well.

"Wait a few minutes before calling on Willa," Beth reminded us.

"No need to worry." Melinda's curly brown hair swayed in the spring breeze, the strands almost as animated as the person they were attached to. "Just make sure to keep your meeting with the duke brief. We will do our best to keep the marquis entertained."

Beth headed out and slipped through a side gate in the wrought iron fence surrounding the estate before giving us one last glance as she sneaked off to the back. Thankfully, there was plenty of foliage and shrubbery obscuring Beth's path around the manor.

"And now we wait," I told Melinda while I smoothed out

my dress. Once multiple carriages had passed us by, and I assumed that Beth should have managed to enter Bambreich Manor, Melinda and I entered through the main gate and strolled up the grand entryway.

Melinda lifted the heavy brass knocker and announced our arrival. The butler greeted us, followed by the Marquis of Bambreich, who strolled down the hallway, seeming pleased to see us.

The marquis tucked one arm against his midriff and bowed towards Melinda and me. "Welcome again. I hope you are looking forward to our outing." He turned towards his butler. "Have you seen Willa? Is she ready yet?"

"I am right here, Papa." Willa strode up behind her father and flashed us a friendly smile.

"Perfect, then I suppose we are almost ready to head out." He turned to the butler. "Could you fetch me my coat and have a carriage called?"

The butler fetched a gray woolen coat from the hall closet and handed it to the marquis.

The marquis slipped on the coat. "Thank you. After you've called for a carriage, you may join the other staff. I am certain they are all clamoring to leave for the circus."

The butler inclined his head. "Thank you, sir."

I moved to Willa's side and leaned towards her, whispering in her ear. "Did Beth manage to get in?"

Willa nodded, meeting my gaze. "Beth will be fine. She's currently holed up in the room of one of my maids." She returned her focus to her father. "I suppose it is up to us now to keep Papa away from home for as long as possible." A small smirk appeared on her face. I could not keep from staring at her full lower lip.

The marquis pulled me from my musings when he grabbed his silver-topped cane and tapped it against the flagstones of the Bambreich Manor foyer. The sound echoed across the spacious entryway. Melinda raked her hand through her curls and returned her loose hair to her back. It appeared as if she was fluttering her lashes at the marquis, but I had to be mistaken; perhaps something got caught in her eye.

Willa's father held out his arm for Melinda, then, once Melinda hooked her arm with his, turned to Willa and me. "Let us venture to the circus."

A forty-minute drive later, we arrived at Astley's Amphitheater. The marquis had arranged a box for us with an excellent view of the ring and stage. A large chandelier hung from the sky-blue ceiling, lighting up the faces of everyone waiting for the show. Bright yellow paint on the viewing boxes gave the inside of the amphitheater a cheerful look. The gallery seats were filled by people from all walks of life, many drinking from tankards of ale as the murmurs of excitement grew.

A couple of years ago, there had been a traveling circus that traveled through Westbridge, which included a puppet show, a strong man, and a peddler of elixirs that claimed to cure anything from baldness to warts. But I had never been to a circus this grand in scale.

The marquis showed Melinda to a velvet seat and settled himself beside her. Willa and I scooted in next to each other on the other two seats. I leaned forward, resting my forearms on the front of the viewing box. I craned my head to gaze around the amphitheater, taking in the decor and the other people attending the show.

The thick black curtains were still drawn. I knew we were here to give Beth enough time to deal with the Irish duke, but I still felt excitement bubbling up inside of me. The sounds of the crowd and the anticipation of seeing the performances were raising my spirits.

Willa, noticing the anticipation on my face, leaned into my side. Her soft curves pressed up against me. "Have you never been before?"

My skin heated where I could feel her pressed against me. I swallowed. "No." All my thoughts about the circus flew out the window, and I became aware of Willa's nearness. What was it about Willa that made me react this way? She made me nervous about being near her, though I still looked forward to seeing her again.

Keeping my eyes trained on the still-empty ring, I was aware of her eyes on me. I should not even be at the circus. There were no eligible bachelors here.

I cursed Beth and her hair-brained schemes. London was supposed to be my chance to find someone to marry and pull my family out of financial ruin, but instead, I sat in an amphitheater while Beth risked her standing in society by deceiving a duke.

I nearly sighed when a high, clear bell rang out, and the heavy black curtains that obscured the stage were lifted. The pressure against my side lessened as Willa scooted to the front of her seat, but her sweet-scented perfume lingered, notes of jasmine and honeysuckle clinging to her skin.

A man strode out onto the stage, accompanied by cheers.

He wore a bright red double-breasted jacket adorned with brass buttons and yellow threaded cords. His top hat was embellished with a similar bright red lining to his jacket. In his hands, he held a whip.

The ringmaster waved the whip through the air, then cracked it loudly on the stage, heightening the fervor of the crowd before slipping the leather almost lovingly through his other hand. His voice bellowed out across the amphitheater as he announced the circus opened.

I could hear the sound of hooves hitting dirt before I saw them appear from the side entrance leading into the ring at the center of Astley's Amphitheater. Two sleek, glossy, black-coated horses trotted out next to each other, heads raised while their rider stood atop their backs, one foot on each of the saddles. I was entranced by the sight. Willa wiggled forward, her bottom lip caught between her teeth.

The marquis and Melinda only had eyes for each other, their faces animated as they chatted with each other. I wondered if the time-traveling woman was doing this solely as a favor to Beth or if she had other motivations. It was clear that she enjoyed the time she spent with the marquis; she had shown a lot of interest in Willa's father during cream tea at Bambreich Manor as well.

"Treats anyone?" A salesman carrying a tray filled with spun sugar and other sweet treats stopped by our box. Willa turned away from the trick riding show below and craned her neck to look at the salesman. Her eyes widened, flashing with excitement. Amused at her reaction, I smiled.

My mind traveled back to Lady Westham's ball when Willa had offered me a mandarin segment. From the few times I had met her, I already deduced that she had a giant sweet tooth. I patted the small reticule in my pocket, its weight unnoticeable since I did not have many coins. Still, I felt the urge to get Willa something.

"Two spun-sugar sticks, please," I told the salesman.

"That'll be sixpence, miss." His mustache bristling, he handed me the two treats while I fished out a coin from my reticule and handed it to him.

Happy with my purchase, I held out one of the sticks to Willa. "For you." She flashed me another of her warm smiles.

"Thank you."

I turned back to gaze at the horses. The trick rider was now doing handstands on the back of a horse as they rode circles around the ring. But from the corner of my eye, I remained aware of Willa. Her fiery hair framed her cheek in soft ringlets as she nipped at the treat in her hands. Seeing her enjoy the sweet warmed my heart.

Pausing, Willa looked at me. "Are you not going to eat yours?"

I had nearly forgotten I also held a treat in my hand, so I quickly took a bite, sugar dissolving on my tongue. Another round of applause sounded across the amphitheater as the trick rider performed an even more difficult stunt.

"Do you think Beth will be able to dissuade the duke?" Willa said, angling herself towards me. She kept her voice low, not quite a whisper but soft enough not to be overheard by her father. Her green eyes were hopeful.

"Perhaps." However, my face must have mirrored my doubts.

"You do not believe so?" Willa immediately retorted.

"I... hope so."

Willa snorted. "That is not the same thing."

"No, it is not," I conceded. "I believe that Beth intends to dissuade the duke, but I am concerned that she may have developed a certain... attachment. She might not mean to encourage him but might unwittingly still do so. You did see how she acted when she returned to us at Lady Westham's ball."

Willa's gaze met mine, green eyes filled with understanding. "I think you are right, though; I suppose we shall see once we've returned." Her brows knitted together. "I just want to be finished with this."

I wanted to reach out and hold her hand. Instead, I asked, "Why do you not want to meet the duke?"

Willa's eyes turned away from me to stare off into the distance. I waited for her response, and when she did finally speak, she sounded older, wearier.

"I feel like Papa has pushed me away ever since Mama's death. Perhaps I remind him too much of her, or perhaps I disappoint him." Her eyes flitted to Melinda and her father, the two of them still engaging in an animated conversation. "It is strange..." she said, trailing off.

"What is strange?"

Willa let out an enervated chuckle. "These past four years, Papa's smiles have been rare, and now, having seen Melinda only twice, I have seen him smile more than those years combined." She frowned for a second before smoothing out her features. "Not that I do not want Papa to smile." She looked at me again. It was plain to see that she wanted me to understand that she did not feel jealous. "I do not know Melinda's intentions, but if she can bring Papa some happiness, then who am I to deny it?"

"She said she was here to help Beth, but I am not so certain." I raised my brow. "I think she might be overlooking the fact that her magical bookshop could have a plan for her." As far as plans from inanimate buildings can go.

Willa nodded. "Perhaps the bookshop is trying to bring Melinda and my Papa together, and Beth has nothing to do with her arrival." She chewed on some more spun sugar until she finished the stick and licked clean the last of the residue. "I want Papa to be happy; I just wish he would stop trying to push me away. I miss her too."

"I am certain your father knows." I considered Willa's words. "Perhaps all your father wants is for you to be happy."

Willa pursed her lips. "Perhaps. But I do not want to marry a man."

I nodded and softly said, "You could try explaining that to your father. He seems like an understanding man."

Willa shrugged and lowered her gaze before switching topics. "What about you?"

"What about me?" The way the light from the chandelier illuminated Willa's tilted face reminded me of a classical painting; her freckles spread out like constellations on her creamy skin. She was breathtaking.

"You said you did not want my help matchmaking, but what are you planning to do?"

"I..." I bit my lip. With Willa this near, I could scarcely think. "My sister, my mother, my brother, they all rely on me marrying. I cannot let them down."

Something undefined flashed across Willa's eyes. I worried

I had disappointed her somehow. Feeling embarrassed, I pulled my gaze away from her and continued watching the show while finishing the rest of my treat.

The rest of the show passed by smoothly, with many other entertaining acts. I just hoped that Beth had had enough time to get rid of the duke when we finally got up to return to Bambreich Manor.

9

Friendship

Back at Bambreich Manor, I thanked the marquis for the outing, then said goodbye to Willa, gaze lingering as I excused myself from their presence. The glossy black cab that had chauffeured us from the circus was still waiting by the curb to take me back to the rented house near Covent Garden. I picked up my pace when my foot hit the stone tread outside the front doors. There had been no sight of Beth when we arrived, but she had to be here. I wondered how it had gone.

When I walked up beside the carriage, the driver leaned over and looked at me, reins readied in his hands. "Where to, miss?"

"Covent Garden," I answered, my gaze moving to the side gate to see if I could see the familiar flash of blonde hair.

The driver nodded and adjusted himself on the bench. "When you are ready…" His gruff voice trailed, hinting at me to enter the carriage.

"Just a moment. I am expecting another. She should be here any moment." As I gazed up at the driver, a metal creak from unoiled hinges came from behind me, and finally, Beth appeared, sneaking through the side gate.

"What took you so long?" I snapped at her, a little harsher than I intended.

A warm bloom blossomed on her cheeks. "I was waiting for Willa." She passed by me and lowered her head to enter the carriage.

I nodded at the driver before entering and closing the door behind me.

"I couldn't very well stand here and wave you on as you returned from the circus, now could I?" Beth continued when I'd taken my place on the bench across from her. She adjusted her skirts and leaned back against the padded wall.

My brows knitted together. "So, how did it go? Is it over?"

Beth chewed her lip, the both of us jostling as the carriage started its path toward home. I feared I knew what was coming based on her lackluster response.

"Really?"

Beth pursed her lips apologetically when she heard the accusation in my voice. "The duke has invited us to go to Covent Garden. I-I want to see him again. There, I've said it." Then her expression changed. Beth tipped her chin and pursed her lip, her arms which were lying loose in her lap, now folded over each other. "I've never had this much excitement in my life, and I will not apologize for wanting to see Edmund again."

Stunned, I looked at Beth. "But he does not know who you are. How do you plan on overcoming that?"

"I do not know yet. Perhaps I will tell him the truth."

"If you are so intent on courting could you not have found another more attainable man?"

Beth looked at me. "No. They would not be Edmund. Would you..." She stopped speaking and shook her head. "Never mind. How about we discuss something else? How was the circus?"

I let out a humph and glanced out the window; the narrow brick buildings of London were hardly visible from behind the curtains. "It was exciting. There were rope walkers and trick riders. Willa and I ate a candied treat." A smile crept up my face as I thought about Willa's various expressions of shock and awe with every stunt. "I had a splendid time when I was not worrying about you."

Beth laughed. "You do not need to worry about me. Everything went smoothly with the duke; he never suspected a thing."

***

I was certain I had developed gray hairs chaperoning Beth and the duke around Covent Garden, especially when we had a near run-in with John and Rose Easton. Beth's brother and sister-in-law would not have been pleased to find out about Beth meeting with strange men and pretending to be someone she was not. But luck had been on our side, and we managed to get away unseen.

"A cauliflower?" Willa laughed when I told her what happened when we were again reunited at Bambreich Manor. A warm feeling bubbled up in my stomach, seeing Willa's face lit up with laughter. She had nestled herself into one of the tufted chairs in the sitting room, her elegant finger twirling a loose thread hanging from one of the throw pillows.

My eyes crinkled from laughing as I recounted the rest of the tale. "Beth patted the cauliflower as if she was patting the head of a child. You should have seen the look on the duke's face."

I hiccupped as I said the last bit. Willa's laughter was infectious, and soon we were grinning. The peals of laughter caused a stitch in my ribcage. I clutched my side and wiped away the wetness below my eyes, composing myself once more.

Beth's lips turned thin as she paced around the room. I joined Willa in a chair beside her.

"What was I supposed to do?" Beth asked. "I could not have my brother see us. Besides, it isn't like there are many places to hide."

Beth's affronted expression threatened to send me into another fit of laughter, so I stroked my cheeks to calm myself, brushing back a few of the stray hairs behind my ears. "He looked so confused." I glanced at Willa and shook my head.

Willa's feline eyes lingered on me before I turned my gaze back to Beth. "I cannot believe he still wants to see you again after that whole debacle. Perhaps he is perfect for you."

"Very funny." Beth's gaze was steely; however, with her soft and friendly appearance, I could not take her seriously when she was scowling.

Melinda strode into the sitting room without an announcement, turning all our gazes toward her.

"Anne might have a point," Melinda said, purple dress fluttering around her full frame. Did I? What point had I made? I tried to remember what I had said when Melinda continued, her eyes flitting to Willa. "Your father asked if I would come to see if you ladies would like to head outside for tea. But..." One of her fingers rested against her chin as if in thought. "While I have you here; I have been thinking that there must be a reason the bookshop sent me to this place. And just now, hearing Anne's words, I realized that perhaps it is to help Beth." Melinda scrutinized Beth. "Perhaps the reason that I am here is to get you and the duke together."

"Wait," Willa said, frowning as she stood. She'd dropped the pillow she had been picking at to the side. "That makes no sense. The duke thinks that Beth is me. Shouldn't she continue to try to get him to break things off?"

Without tilting her head, Melinda's eyes flashed to Beth. "There might be another way. But first, Beth, do you like him?"

Beth had stopped pacing and stared at Melinda. I could tell that her mind was racing, though I had a feeling that I knew what she was about to say. Her reaction in the carriage, after I returned from the circus, had been enough of a confirmation. Beth was infatuated with the duke.

I huffed and stared at Melinda. This time-traveling woman had no business interfering in other people's lives. I had made John Easton a promise to look out for Beth, and I had not done a good job so far. I felt guilty for that, especially with how kindly he and Rose had treated me.

"You do not know why you are here," I told Melinda. "It could have nothing to do with Beth." My gaze flitted to Willa, who tipped her head at me and smiled, cocking a brow. I straightened my posture and remained firm. "This started as a way to help Willa. So perhaps we need to figure out how to get the duke to return to Ireland."

Willa walked over to me and clasped my hand, threading her warm fingers with mine. A tingle shot up my spine at the contact.

Once again, Willa smiled at me, taking my breath away. "Thank you for thinking of me." The pressure of her hand on mine increased. "Though as long as the outcome is that I remain unmarried, I am open to other suggestions. I may have started this whole mess, but what is it that you want, Beth?" Willa glanced at my friend, who stood hesitating on the sideline.

"I do not know. Does it even matter whether I like him? This entire time he has been under the impression that he has been spending time with the daughter of a marquis. If he knew the real me, he might not like me. My brother might be wealthy, but he does not have a title. What if marrying someone with a title is all the duke cares about?"

Willa shifted beside me. "Then it is his loss."

"And what if he feels the same?" Melinda stared at Beth with a straight face.

I held my breath as Beth answered bluntly, "I think you have intervened in enough people's lives; I do not need any assistance." She strode towards the settee and dropped herself down into its plush cushions. Her chest heaved, and her expression turned melancholic. "He is not going to want me once he finds out. I cannot tell him now."

Willa shrugged, letting go of my hand. A pang of loss rang through me; her nearness was a comfort, and whenever she touched me, I ached for more.

Willa straightened, her voice direct. "Then do not tell the duke yet. Continue courting him and wait for the right time."

"When would that be?" Beth said, biting her lip.

I crossed my arms. I was fed up with everyone's folly. "Beth, you aren't considering continuing with this charade, are you? What about your brother and Rose? You came so close to being caught today."

Beth's tone rose. "But I was not, and hopefully, next time, the duke will take me somewhere further away from our London rental house."

Melinda nodded sagely, as if she wasn't playing the part of the instigator. "So, you have decided?" Beth nodded. "All right, let's get to matchmaking."

Melinda had gotten what she wanted and now led us from the sitting room towards the side garden where Willa's father was waiting at a table laden with a full cream tea spread. As soon as he noticed Melinda's return, he stood hastily, patting off his lapel, and bowed towards us.

"Please," he said with a sweep of his arm, motioning at the empty seats surrounding the table. "I hope you all have an appetite."

The weather was pleasant, with a faint breeze disturbing the rhododendrons planted alongside the manor. The butler was nowhere in sight, so we helped ourselves, pouring tea into delicate cups and sharing plates of rolled dates, biscuits, and fruits with each other. The marquis was having an upbeat conversation with Melinda on one side while I scooted in beside Willa on the opposite side.

Willa stirred some sugar into her tea and took a sip. Observing her father and Melinda again, I turned to Willa.

"I do not think Melinda is here for Beth. If her bookshop is meant to be intuitive, perhaps the one needing love is her."

Willa tilted her face towards me, her voice a sweet whisper. "You think my father and Melinda..." She frowned slightly, looking at the two of them. "Are growing closer?"

I followed her gaze, seeing the marquis smile broadly as Melinda spoke, refilling her cup the instant it was emptied. "Can you deny it?"

Willa shifted, her eyes back on me. "No, I cannot."

"It is obvious they have grown fond of each other, though I wonder whether Melinda has realized what it might mean. I think she might be too blinded by Beth and the duke."

Picking up one of the dates, Willa took a bite and chewed thoughtfully. "It must be lonely—"

"Lonely?" I watched Willa chew and swallow, waiting for her to continue.

"Think about it," she said after rinsing away the food with a mouthful of tea. "She is the owner of this magical book-shop, traveling through time by herself, helping others find their soulmates. Sure, it must be exciting to bring others their happy endings the first few years but after that? When it is always everyone else finding love and never her?" Willa gazed at me. I nearly squirmed under her scrutinizing eyes. "I do not think I could do it."

"I wonder how long she has been the owner of the book-shop." Willa's words made me realize how little we knew about Melinda. We did not ask many questions, but in turn, she also remained vague in her answers. I shied away from inquiring since it was too far outside my knowledge.

"Perhaps it would not be the worst thing if Melinda and

my father found happiness with each other. As long as she does not lead my father on," Willa said, a hint of protectiveness flavoring her words. "And perhaps you can go easy on Beth? You can protect her without being overbearing." Willa's lip lifted into a smile when she caught my abashed face. "What do you think?"

"Perhaps..." I hesitated, chewing my lip. "But I owe her and her brother much."

Beth, unaware that Willa and I were discussing her, nibbled on a biscuit. Some words Beth had said to me when we were on the outing at Covent Garden came to mind. She had questioned me about finding a suitor and whether I had changed my mind, alluding to the fact that I might be harboring some feelings for someone of my own.

I had swiftly denied those claims, of course. Willa and I were friends, that's all. And yet... I mulled over Beth's words. Was it friendship that made my heart race whenever Willa was near? Friendship that made me yearn to feel her touch, however fleeting? Friendship that brightened my spirits whenever I knew I would see her?

I felt conflicted. I did not know if Willa even thought of me. And I had no business in regards to Willa when the sole reason for me being in London was to find a suitor to marry. I could not let my family down. If I failed to secure a marriage, then my sister might have to marry someone she did not love; I could not let that happen.

It had to be me.

10

Wallflowers

Between another outing with Beth and the duke at the Foundling Hospital and passing the time with John and Rose Easton, it had been a few days since I had seen Willa. I missed seeing her freckled face and hearing her perky voice. Her outspokenness always cheered me up. Thankfully, my day got brighter when Willa showed up mid-morning at the Eastons' rented house near Covent Garden.

Rose led Willa into the back garden, where Beth and I were drinking tea. The butler was hovering behind us since he had only just ordered one of the maids to bring us cups and saucers.

"Please, take a seat and enjoy yourself. It is nice to meet you," Rose said. She waved at us and returned inside, most likely to join John in the study.

The butler moved to action, pulling out a chair beside me and waiting for Willa to sit before pushing it back in. "I will leave you to it, Ms. Easton and Ms. Blakeley," he said, inclining his head.

"Thank you, Bartley. Perhaps you could ask Mary to bring out another cup and more tea?" Beth said.

The butler was ever the professional as he moved to the servants' quarter.

It was a nice surprise to see Willa when I wasn't expecting her. She looked fresh in a pale green day dress that reminded me of the first shoots of grass crawling up out of the soil after a long winter. However, her red hair was a bit disheveled, snarls of hair curling up as if she had rushed out of Bambreich Manor without combing her hair.

Willa barely said hello before diving into her reason for visiting. "You will have to come to the Farnsby's ball with me."

Beth set down her cup and leaned forward. "Now, what were you saying about a ball?"

"The duke sent a letter to my father asking if I would join him at the Farnsby's ball. I was not able to lift it from the stack of correspondence before my father had already opened it." Willa's brows knitted together, her gaze stuck on Beth.

"When is it?"

Willa turned to the side. "This evening. I will have to return home soon because my father is excited that I received an invitation and wants to see me dressed properly." Her eyes moved to Beth again, pleading. "You can come, can't you? The duke will be expecting to see you there."

Beth immediately assuaged Willa's worry. "Yes, of course."

Willa visibly relaxed as the tension left her shoulders, then she returned her attention to me. "You are coming as well, I hope? I need someone to keep me company while Beth is off flirting with the duke." Her voice sounded hopeful, but I wondered if I was inferring meanings from her words that were not there. Perhaps I was only an afterthought now that the immediate threat had subsided. Regardless, I was not going to turn down her invitation.

I nodded, a smile on my face. "I will be there."

"Good. The ball starts at eight."

***

Beth busied herself worrying about what to wear to the Farnsby's ball while I could only think about seeing Willa again. Was I supposed to also look for eligible bachelors? Sure. But that remained an afterthought when we entered the candlelit ballroom and I spotted Willa.

I grinned when I noticed she was once again standing near the refreshments, her red hair glowing like flames wherever the flicker of a candle cast its light. She'd traded in her day dress for a silken moss-green gown that made her appear fey.

Perhaps she was a fairy, cunning and clever and full of tricks with the way she mesmerized me. She had not yet seen me, and I savored the moment to watch her as she stood by herself. She twirled a lock of curly hair with her finger as she absentmindedly nibbled on something. She was too far away for me to see just what it was that she was eating.

Beth nudged me. "I see Edmund. Will you tell Willa I said hello?"

"I will. Be careful and have fun." Then I crossed the room, heading straight for Willa. She chewed and swayed to the music, turning to gaze around the room. Her eyes widened when she saw me walking towards her, and she immediately waved at me and motioned me over.

"Did Beth find the duke already?" she asked.

I nodded and pointed toward the dance floor, where the two of them had already positioned themselves in between other dancing couples.

"Beth can't take her eyes off him." Willa smirked, shaking her head.

"Nor her hands." I rolled my eyes and received an amused snort from Willa.

She lifted her brow. "You still do not approve?"

"I think it is risky, but it is Beth's choice."

Willa nodded and brushed up against my arm as she moved in closer. Honeysuckle and jasmine once again floated around my face. I practically dreamed of the scent. She gazed up at me, her upper teeth gently biting her full upper lip. I felt the urge to reach out and trace the shape of her mouth with my thumb but managed to keep my hand to my side, aware of my surroundings. Perhaps Willa saw something in my eyes because she swallowed roughly before letting out a throaty chuckle.

"Are you hungry?" She pointed at the hors d'oeuvres.

"I could eat." Willa grabbed a cracker topped with caviar; her lashes lowered as she handed it to me. I noticed the attractive flush tinting her neck and face. My fingers brushed hers as I accepted the cracker and ate it. Willa followed suit, stuffing an entire cracker into her mouth, then regretting it immediately. I was bemused by her behavior. Was she reacting to me? But before I could say anything, Beth had returned from dancing with the duke. I regretted the intrusion.

Willa cleared her throat and swallowed the bit of food. "Beth, good effort keeping your hands away from each other."

I turned to the refreshments and picked another cracker from the tiered stand on top of the table, handing it to Willa.

She flashed me a smile. "Thank you." I smiled back before addressing Beth.

"Willa has a point. He looked as if he was going to kiss you right then and there. The scandal if that would have happened."

Beth paled and glanced around the room before lowering her voice, though she managed to keep some bite to her words. "Anne, you do not need to announce it to the entire room. Lower your voice."

Willa snorted as she chewed the hors d'oeuvre I had given her. With a bit of righteous indignation, I pointed at the guests filling the ballroom; none of the Farnsby's guests spared us a second glance. "Everyone is too preoccupied with dancing and drinking to pay attention to us wallflowers."

"Still..." Beth huddled in closer. "Edmund did ask to speak to me later this evening. He said he would come and find me. I wonder what he wants to tell me."

Sometimes Beth could be so oblivious. The duke had sent a letter to Willa's home, inviting her to this ball specifically. By my mental calculations, he was infatuated with Beth and wanted to ask for her hand in marriage. "You cannot tell me you have no idea what he wants to tell you," I said.

Beth looked worried. Her hands fidgeted with the side seam of her dress. "It cannot be, not yet. I have not told him the truth."

Willa shrugged, showing concern. "Yes, but he does not

know that. He is under the impression that you are me and that my father is not only encouraging the match but indeed actively seeking it out."

"And he likes you," I said, agreeing with Willa's words.

Beth frowned and turned to fidgeting with the ribbon around her waist. "Fair point," she shot out reluctantly. "What am I supposed to do? I cannot let him propose without knowing the truth."

I did not like to see Beth worried. Pursing my lips as I thought, I decided that the best method would have to be honesty. There was no path forward for Beth and the duke unless the truth was laid bare.

I nodded to Beth. "When he takes you somewhere private, you should ask to speak first. Tell him the truth. It will be up to the duke whether he accepts your apology, but at least he will know the truth, and so will you. If he loves you, he will make the right decision. And if he does not, then you will be better off without him."

My heart ached as I said those words to Beth. At least she was honest about her feelings toward the duke, and perhaps he would love her for who she was. I could not deceive myself either; I was developing feelings for Willa. But could I hope for them to be reciprocated? Willa was outgoing and outspoken in a way that I was not. Perhaps all the signs I saw, the flustered glances and touches that lingered just a tad longer than usual, were mere fabrications of my imagination.

I pushed my thoughts aside and squeezed Beth's hand. "I think you need something to fortify yourself with." But the one who needed something to soothe her frayed nerves was me. I glanced around the room, trying to spot one of the circulating servers. I found one, a young man wearing solid black, carrying a tray of glasses filled with punch.

11

Fleeting Dance

Returning to Beth and Willa's side, I handed them both a glass before tipping back the one I got for myself. The drink packed a punch, liquor as thick and sweet as syrup gliding down my throat.

Willa hissed as she swallowed a sip. "That is one of the strongest glasses of punch I have encountered. By my count, half of those attending shall be deep within their cups and snoring in their chairs before long."

Beth drank deep before gazing longingly at the couples dancing, her mind most likely pondering the duke again. "Perhaps we could take some air to clear my head?" she said, averting her eyes with a troubled look.

Willa and I glanced at each other and then nodded.

"Of course," Willa said. Beth moved first, winding her way past the mingling couples and men introducing themselves to other ladies. I wondered if I should stay and put in more effort to meet with them. But then Willa grasped my hand and pulled me along, leaving the laughter and loud chatter behind. Passing through the side door, we stepped outdoors, crisp, fragrant night air blowing away the mingled smells of foods and people congregating. Muffled music and the soft murmurs of guests could still be heard, but it was quieter, more peaceful.

Beth pulled a handkerchief from her pocket and patted the sides of her flushed face. Willa still held my hand and led me to a wooden bench, burning torches accentuating the gravel pathways and decorative bushes. Beth joined us once she finished patting her cheeks.

"Where is Melinda?" Beth asked Willa. "I have not seen her in a while." Beth and I had not been at Bambreich Manor for a couple of days, so we had not heard anything from Melinda.

Willa snorted, shaking the bench. "She has taken a liking to my father and is occupying a lot of his time."

"That is a good thing... right?"

Willa rolled her eyes. "It is." I knew Willa still had reservations about the time-traveling woman, especially when that woman was getting closer to her father. "I like Melinda," Willa continued. "She is a bit of an odd duck, but she is kind. And having her around to distract my father is also beneficial. Without her, our scheme more than likely would have been found out already. My father is not stupid." Willa stopped, taking in a deep breath. Her gaze turned to me, and in a soft voice, she added, "I have also enjoyed spending time with you."

I had to remind myself that Willa meant both Beth and me, not just me, though my cheeks started burning. It could have been a trick of the light, but her eyes seemed to want to convey something to me.

I could not keep staring at Willa, so I cleared my throat and averted my eyes.

Willa took my reaction in stride and smiled wistfully. "However, it is strange to see my father hanging onto every word of another woman. He has been so different. I cannot recall the last time I saw him smile like this. It worries me as well since Melinda is...." No one was around to eavesdrop on our conversation, but Willa still lowered her voice. "A time-traveler."

I nodded.

"I am worried that he will be hurt when she eventually leaves."

Beth tapped her hand against her legs. "Has Melinda said she was leaving?"

"Not yet." Willa shifted her weight and crossed her legs.

"Then perhaps you could ask her when you see her next. It might alleviate your worries."

"I suppose," Willa answered Beth with reluctance.

I laid my hand on Willa's arm, trying to soothe her feelings. "Would you like me to be there when you do?"

The crease between Willa's brows released, and her green eyes softened, a grateful smile forming on her lips. "I would." She sighed, breathing out the tension in her body, lowering her taut shoulders, and smacking the side of her thigh. "All right, let us take a turn about the garden. It is getting a bit cold sitting still."

I glanced at her bare arms, and a thin layer of goosebumps

indeed covered her skin. Fine hairs raised and shimmered in the firelight. "Would you rather return indoors?"

At least there, we would be warmed by the presence of the gathered guests and the roaring fire in the fireplace warming the massive ballroom. Before waiting for Willa's answer, I slipped the shawl I was wearing off my shoulders and fastened it around her shoulders, my touch lingering at her nape, which felt like ice.

"Not yet," Willa said as she adjusted my shawl. Music from indoors drifted out on the wind, adding a liveliness to the evening sky.

Willa grasped my hand as she stood from the bench, her face tipped skyward, long lashes brushing her freckled cheeks as she closed her eyes. She swayed softly to the piano chords. Was it a waltz being played? I couldn't quite recognize the melody, but seeing Willa enjoying herself ignited something within me. Her closed eyes gave me the excuse to stare at her without worrying about seeming odd.

Willa's grasp, at first soft and gentle, turned more insistent as she pulled me closer. She placed her other hand on my side, offering me a gentle smile that stirred my heart as she opened her eyes once more. Why did I only feel this way with Willa? I mulled it over before I remembered that it wasn't just the two of us here. Where was Beth? I glanced to the side for my friend, but without noticing, she had left the two of us alone.

I briefly wondered if Beth returned inside to find the duke, but all thoughts about her dissipated as soon as I heard Willa's low whisper, my gaze whipping back to her freckled face.

"I've been wanting to dance with you all evening."

"You have?" My swaying jarred. My palms felt slippery

and sweaty despite the cool air. I just hoped Willa would not notice.

Willa nodded, her hold on my hip searing into my flesh. She looked too good to be true with my shawl draped around her shoulders. Her green eyes were on me. "It is why I did not want to go inside. We couldn't—I couldn't..." Willa chewed her lip, hesitating as her hand fisted the fabric on my waist. "I have been... happier since I've met you."

I swallowed to clear my throat. My skin buzzed at her words. Willa was happier? Did she mean... But I stopped my train of thought. I did not want to presume what she meant. Willa looked up at me, waiting.

"I have been happier too."

Willa nodded, a rosiness creeping into her pale cheeks. She leaned in closer to me as we continued our dance, well out of view from anyone indoors. The night air helped cool the fever burning inside me as Willa was cradled in my arms, swaying in time with the music; only the soft murmurs from the guests inside reminded us that we were not alone.

I parted my lips to say more. My hand itched to reach out and cradle her face, but the sound of feet hitting gravel rang across the yard, and Willa and I broke apart in a hurry. The rushed steps were headed straight for us. My cheeks burned as we finally stood an appropriate distance away. Willa and I glanced back to see Beth darting around the corner, clutching her dress to keep the fabric from dragging, face drawn. When she got closer, I could tell she was crying, tear tracks marking her ashen cheeks.

"What happened?" I asked, spurring into motion. I looked

Beth up and down and grabbed her face to see if anyone had hurt her.

"The duke knows," Beth bit out. Her brows knitted together, a wet sheen shimmering across her eyes. Using my thumb, I wiped away the wetness beneath her eyes.

"Did you tell him?" A look of concern crossed Willa's face as she joined my side.

Beth shook her head. "I did not have the chance."

"Then how?"

Beth sighed, choking back a sob. "Arabella Brocklehurst showed up calling my name. After that, I had no choice but to come clean. Edmund took one look at me and said goodbye. He—" Beth choked out. "He wants nothing more to do with me."

I pulled Beth into a hug, feeling her shiver against my shoulder. I flashed Willa an apologetic look. "I can't let anyone see Beth like this; I'd better bring her home." I regretted that the night had ended so abruptly. If I had the chance, I would have lingered in Willa's presence for as long as I could, but I needed to take care of my friend. Beth needed me. However, I wondered what could have happened if there had been more time.

"Of course," Willa said, her face neutral. "Come, I will help make sure the way is clear. Let us go back the way she came so no one will see us leave. There should not be any other guests near the front entrance just yet. I will thank Lady Farnsby on your behalf after you both have left."

Willa took the lead, checking around every corner before waving us on. Beth could walk on her own, though she remained silent, her gaze drawn within herself as she stuck to my side. I nudged her on.

"Thank you," I told Willa once we had reached the sidewalk in front of Farnsby's Manor and she had flagged over a carriage. My voice was low and deep as I tried to imbue my words with as much meaning as possible. "Thank you for tonight."

Willa nodded, elegant fingers brushing her arm as she hesitated. "Take care of Beth, and let me know what happens. I—" The tips of her fingers skated along the edge of my shawl that was still draped around her shoulders until she glanced up in surprise. "Oh, this is yours. You should take it back." She moved her hand to pull the fabric back, but I stopped her.

"Keep it."

Willa nodded again and lowered her hand. "I hope I will see you both soon. Hurry on home, and I will excuse you with Lady Farnsby."

12

Suitors

First, I had been too busy chaperoning Beth and supporting both her and Willa with their scheme to mislead the duke. Then I spent a few days consoling a heartbroken Beth because the duke turned away from her after finding out she had been lying about her identity. I rebuked myself for losing sight of my purpose for being in London. I still needed to attract someone willing to marry me.

I was glad that Beth had turned a new leaf and traded in her sulking for an air of defiance, sending her French maid and the driver out for errands. I worried a bit about her sudden change of attitude, but her insistence on hosting suitors was an opportunity I could not let slip.

After she returned from running errands, Estelle worked magic on our hair. Beth looked beautiful and rosy-cheeked in a pink dress, with her hair wound into a circular pattern. My features were harsher, more austere; of all my siblings, I took most after my mother.

Randolph took after our father with hair the color of wheat and a bright, friendly face, whereas Mary still had the chestnut hair though Mama's severe bone structure appeared more delicate on her. Estelle had done a marvelous job softening my face with elegantly placed curls and a sweeping knot on the crown of my head.

Before long, Beth and I sat next to each other in the drawing room, waiting for the three suitors to arrive. Rose had taken a seat towards the corner, playing the role of chaperon.

Beth had arranged for quite a spread of refreshments; the table in front of us was laden with crackers and tarts, as well as lemonade. Willa would have loved one of those tarts. I smiled at the thought of her trying foods wherever she went. I had never met anyone with such a sweet tooth.

Beside me, Beth sat up straight, her back as stiff as a post and her lip trembling. Although this had been Beth's idea, she did not look happy about it. I wondered if I should ask if she was all right when Rose stood, concern painted across her face.

"Are you sure you want to do this? I don't know what is going on with you, but you don't look like you are excited about having suitors over."

Beth, without blinking an eye, answered, "Thank you, Rose, but I am all right. Perhaps a bit nervous, but that shall pass soon enough."

I could tell Rose did not believe Beth, but she still said, "Okay then. I'll let Bartley know that you are ready."

"Thank you."

I caught a flicker of hurt in Rose's eyes before she turned away and left the drawing room to fetch the butler. Rose and Beth were normally very close, so it pained me to see Beth keeping things from her. I knew Beth worried about her brother's reaction; he would not be pleased if he ever found out about the risks she had been taking. But Rose deserved to know. Perhaps I needed to talk some sense into Beth.

"I believe I understand why you have not told Rose anything, but she is your friend as well as your sister-in-law. Does she not deserve to know?"

Beth blushed and glanced down at her hands. "I do not know how to bring it up to Rose, and she would be obligated to tell my brother. I could not bear him finding out. You do not need to worry about me. It is over between me and the duke, and I am making sure that my feelings shall be well and buried in the past."

I managed to control my expression though I wanted to raise my brow at Beth. The hurt in her voice rang through undisguised, and I knew she was nowhere near finished with the duke.

"Just think things through," I said, worrying that Beth would overcompensate and throw herself into a liaison with one of the suitors visiting today. I wanted to say more but was interrupted by the butler's deep voice as he entered the drawing room with the first suitor in tow.

"Mr. Eddington," Bartley announced, directing the suitor to one of the open chairs opposite us.

Mr. Eddington took a few steps forward before clamping his legs shut and bowing forward, making a grand gesture as he pulled one of his arms behind his back. His face turned quite red before moving back to his former stance, his cravat nearly slicing into his neck—a washerwoman must have been heavy-handed with the starch.

"Ms. Easton and Ms. Blakeley, thank you for inviting me into your home on this fine day."

"The pleasure is all mine," Beth said. "Please, have a seat and feel free to take some refreshments."

As I sat there, surrounded by the chatter and laughter of the suitors, a part of me couldn't help but feel a sense of detachment from the whole affair. Beth, my dear friend, was thoroughly engaged in the conversations, her eyes sparkling with excitement and anticipation. But for me, it was different. I couldn't shake off the overwhelming feeling of indifference that washed over me.

Mr. Eddington, Mr. Lovett, and Mr. Garret, the three suitors who had come to visit, each vying for Beth's attention, tried their best to impress us with their charm and wit. They showered us with compliments, their words filled with empty promises and rehearsed flattery. Yet, despite their efforts, I found myself struggling to summon even a hint of interest in their presence.

I glanced at Beth, her smile radiant as she engaged in conversation with Mr. Eddington, her eyes shining with hope. She had been so eager for this day, dreaming of finding a suitable match who could provide her with a secure future. I couldn't help but feel a twinge of guilt for not sharing in her enthusiasm.

My mind wandered, and I found myself questioning the path I was on. Was this what I wanted? Or was I simply going through the motions, trying to please my family and fulfill the expectations set upon me? The Eastons had been kind and generous, inviting me to stay with them in London and supporting me in my pursuit of a wealthy suitor. I owed them a debt of gratitude, and yet, I couldn't deny the growing sense of unease within me.

As the suitors continued their attempts to win our favor, I discreetly observed their actions and listened to their words. But none of it resonated with me. The conversation felt superficial, lacking depth and sincerity. It was as if I were watching a carefully choreographed dance, one in which I had no desire to participate.

My thoughts drifted to the moments of freedom and authenticity I had experienced outside the confines of this marriage market and the moments spent exploring the streets of London with Beth, our laughter echoing through the bustling city. The times when I could be myself without the weight of expectations and societal pressures pressing down on me.

A pang of guilt gripped my heart as I considered the sacrifices made on my behalf. The expensive dresses and accessories and the time and effort invested in presenting me as an eligible young lady. It felt like a charade, a façade I was maintaining for the sake of others.

I took a deep breath, trying to steady my thoughts and find clarity amidst the chaos of emotions. It was time for me to confront my truth and dare to question the path laid out before me. I owed it to myself to find my happiness, to break free from the chains of obligation and expectation.

But for now, I would continue to play my part, to smile and nod politely, concealing the turmoil within. Because the road to self-discovery was not always straightforward, and sometimes we had to navigate through the darkness before finding the light. And so, I remained, grappling with my desires, searching for the courage to forge a path that was truly my own.

13

The Taste Of Oranges

A few days later, I was headed to a soiree at Mr. Alcott's home with Rose and John Easton. Mr. Alcott was a retired naval captain who had been an acquaintance of John and Beth's parents. According to John, he was a bit of an odd duck who, despite his military background, preferred to be called Mister since his retirement.

Beth had declined to go, claiming she did not feel well and wanted to stay in bed. I did not believe her excuse—there had to be more to her staying home. But I was looking forward to the soirée since Willa was attending as well.

Mr. Alcott's home, an older, modest-style home built from dark stonework, was located on the outskirts of London. The place had a rural vibe, more akin to the homes and spacious green fields I was acquainted with in Westbridge.

John, Rose, and I were welcomed into the entryway, where one wainscoted back wall displayed the many military memorabilia Mr. Alcott had collected over the years. I gazed at the mounted bicorn captain's hat, a brass telescope gone green around the edges, and various vibrantly striped and colored ribbons of which I had no way of knowing what they were for. A footman accepted John's outer coat and Rose's shawl.

I had worn a long-sleeved taffeta dress and did not need a shawl or coat to keep the cool bite of the English spring evening at bay. The night air had done wonders for my complexion, bringing a rosiness to my cheeks that was not usually there.

"Right this way," the footman said after he stored away John and Rose's belongings, directing us through the archway towards the back of the house. When we entered the drawing room, an older man with thick, gray sideburns and thinner but equally silvered hair turned towards us. His face lit up, and a jovial smile appeared.

"John, my boy," he said, stretching out his arms. "It has been too long since I have seen you. Let me think... you must have been about twelve. No, thirteen." Mr. Alcott shook his head as he corrected himself. He patted John's left shoulder with his wrinkled hands. "Let me have a good look at you and see how you've grown up." Mr. Alcott adjusted John's waistcoat, taking in his measure. "My, you are the spitting image of your father. It is as if I am looking at his painting."

John smiled. "I have been told that my father and I share a striking resemblance. It's the nose and jaw."

While the others were speaking, I gazed about the room, spotting Willa near a black lacquered pianoforte. A painting of, presumably, a much younger Mr. Alcott in full naval captain attire hung behind her. Willa winked at me with a teasing smile playing on her lips, jolting my heart.

In front of me, Mr. Alcott nodded to John. "And the eyes." His voice trailed for a moment. "But the hair is all your darling mother. Such a wonderful creature she was." He stared at John's hairline before tearing his gaze away, eyes cloudier than before, revealing a hint of mist. "Such an awful thing to have happened to two so young." Inhaling, Mr. Alcott continued, "Och, hear me rambling on and on without welcoming your other companions." He nodded to Rose. "This must be your lovely wife?"

"Yes, this is Rose," John said, grabbing his wife's hand.

Rose smiled at Mr. Alcott, executing a small curtsy, as she said, "It is nice to meet you, Mr. Alcott."

"It is my pleasure, my dear," the old naval captain said. Then he turned to me, looking hesitant. "And this must be your sister?" He glanced back at John for confirmation.

"Unfortunately, my sister did not feel well tonight, so she has decided to stay home and rest; I hope you'll forgive her absence." John pointed to me. "This is Ms. Blakeley, a friend and chaperone to my sister. I am sponsoring her season this year."

"How wonderful to have you visit my home, Ms. Blakeley," Mr. Alcott said to me. "Your last name sounds familiar; perhaps I've met your father before—sturdy man, likes to hunt?"

"Ms. Blakeley and her family also live in Westbridge, so you have likely seen her late father in town on one of your visits with my family," John provided.

Mr. Alcott paused at John's mention of my father and lowered his head. "My condolences, Ms. Blakeley."

"Thank you, sir," I said. "It has been a few years now since his passing."

"Still, the loss of a parent is no small matter." Mr. Alcott's gravelly voice comforted me. "But please, make yourselves comfortable and mingle with the other guests. I am certain John and I can reminisce a bit, and there's also a musician visiting." Mr. Alcott waved over a sprightly man who looked to be in his early thirties. "Murphy, let me introduce you to some friends of mine." The musician joined Mr. Alcott's side with a bright smile.

"Murphy plays the flute," Mr. Alcott said.

"I can't wait to hear you play a song," Rose told Murphy. I tapped on her shoulder once the musician started discussing the tunes in his repertoire and leaned in closer. "I am going to say hello to Willa."

Rose nodded. "Go ahead. I'll say hi in a bit."

I nodded at the other guests mingling in the drawing room. Willa had just finished speaking to a middle-aged woman when I caught up with her. In my excitement to see her, my thoughts stumbled, and I uttered a lame "Hello," cursing myself that I had not managed to say something more interesting.

Willa's eyes crinkled, softening her gaze. "Hello." Her lips rounded softly, seductively. My cheeks heated, and I worried for a moment that the other guests could tell what I was thinking.

The way my body reacted to Willa was foreign to me; a heightening of sensations and emotions, part excitement, part fear. I both wanted to pull her towards me and push her away. What concerned me the most was that I had never even remotely felt anything similar toward a man.

If I tried to focus on their positive attributes, I could perhaps manage to feel some kind of affection towards them but nothing that would spark a fire in my soul the way that Willa did. Only her presence burned through me like an inferno.

Willa turned her head sideways, looking down at the pianoforte, then tapped her finger against the lacquered wood. "Do you like to play?"

"I do." I enjoyed music and loved bringing something as simple as notes on paper to life with my own hands.

"Will you play a song?" Willa smiled coyly, angling her body against the heavy instrument.

"How could I refuse?" I moved to the bench and picked up the stack of sheet music, rifling through to pick a song when Willa slid in beside me, her soft thigh squeezing against mine.

"How about we play together?"

I swallowed, clearing my throat. The other guests noticed us getting ready to play and joined in a circle surrounding the piano. I continued picking through the sheet music when Willa stopped my hand.

"What about this one?"

"'The Magic Flute'?" I turned to Willa. "That is a challenging piece to play..."

"I can handle it," she said, a small smirk appearing on her face. "Can you?" Her eyes challenged me, and I gladly accepted. She had to press in even tighter, the scent of her perfume rising from her collarbone, making me lightheaded.

Willa started us off, and I followed, both of us pressing the keys like a duel. We shot glances at each other as we crossed and uncrossed our arms, our bodies pressing and squeezing against each other as we played the notes. Her cheek skimmed mine, and my fingers fumbled a passage, letting out a false note. But I managed to recover, meeting Willa key for key until we reached the end, our faces flushed. We laughed at each other.

The other guests clapped, and Mr. Alcott brought forward Murphy, the flute player.

"That was some fine playing," the musician said.

"Thank you," Willa said, standing up from the bench. "I suppose we have warmed the crowd up for you," she jested.

"Indeed, indeed," Murphy said, pulling out his flute.

I stood as well and followed Willa toward the back of the drawing room.

"Well, now that everyone is in the mood for some music... do we have any requests?" Murphy asked the other guests. He lifted the flute to his lips and played a quick merry tune before lowering it and waiting for answers.

"'All the Blue Bonnets Are Over the Border,'" an older man called out.

"How about 'Comin Thru the Rye'?" the woman that had been speaking to Willa said.

Willa squeezed my hand then leaned in and whispered against my ear. "Follow me while they are distracted with the flute player." She paused for a moment to gauge my response, but I nodded my head immediately, earning another smile from her.

Willa led us back through the doorway from where I had entered the drawing room. She directed me further along the hallway towards the back of the house. There, she grabbed the handle of a door that appeared to be located on an exterior wall, opening it up to reveal a hothouse.

Tall glass sidings let in a view of the night sky. The moon was full and bright, casting a soft glow on the plants inside. Notes of citrus and something herby mingled in the air. I detected its origin to be the orange trees standing proud at the center, branches loaded with orange globes.

"Look, they are bearing fruit this early in the year."

Willa grinned up at me in delight. She reached out to one of the branches and plucked a ripe orange from between the green leaves. With her dress billowing around her and her red curls wild around her face, she looked ethereal, like a nymph prancing around in the woods. I wondered if I should check the ground for fairy circles.

Thumb pressing in at the top, she peeled part of the orange and slid a segment into her mouth. I watched her chew, the small pink tip of her tongue flicking out to lick the corner of her lip. I recalled Lady Westham's ball, where she had offered me a segment of mandarin.

Orange juices stained her fingertips, and she slowly licked those clean as well. I was breathless as I stared at her. Nothing out of the ordinary was happening, but between our piano duet and her leading me to this empty hot house, I could feel the atmosphere between us changing, turning heady.

Willa gazed up at me, a smile forming on her lips, and she dropped the hand holding the orange to her side. She moved towards me, closing the distance between us until she stood so near, I could count the freckles on her face. Her left hand grazed my waist, and she tipped her face up, green eyes meeting mine.

"Anne," she whispered, her gaze searching for something on my face. My heart raced, and I blushed, unable to speak. But before I knew it, her warm lips pressed against mine. She dropped the orange to the ground and lifted her hand to my face. She cradled my cheek as her mouth moved against mine. My scalp tingled, sending searing tremors down my spine. I needed more. Since I'd met her, I hadn't been able to stop thinking about her. Kissing Willa felt desperate, as if I was drinking the first sip of water after I had been dying of thirst.

Coaxing her lips open, I tasted the orange on her tongue. Happiness and excitement flooded my thoughts; I couldn't believe she felt the same about me. I pulled my arm around her, fingers tightening against her dress, touching the soft dip of her hip. I didn't think I would ever tire of kissing Willa. Her soft puffs of breath against my skin, the slide of our tongues, and the small noises she made in the back of her throat were a revelation.

She was so incredibly beautiful.

A door creaked behind us. I pulled back.

Willa looked at me, her face and chest flushed a delightful pink, but her eyes had gone round, and her brows knitted together. "What now?" Worry tinged every syllable.

Thoughts racing, I grabbed her hand and pulled her to a workbench. Stacks of small crates and various pots stood beside it. We ducked underneath, and I pulled some crates in front of the bench to obscure us from sight.

I squeezed Willa's hand as the door swung open, revealing Mr. Alcott and a few other guests. The hothouse was dark, so I hoped the crates would be enough to keep us from being discovered.

"These are my orange trees, the pride and joy of my Orangerie. I am very proud of them and am delighted that they produce fruit all year round," Mr. Alcott told his guests. We held our breaths as a woman stepped up to admire the orange trees, a foot kicking against the orange that Willa had dropped.

"What is this?" she said, bending over and picking up the partially eaten fruit.

"Perhaps it fell from the tree," Mr. Alcott said.

The woman turned the orange in her hands. "It's missing some peel and a piece of orange. It did not just fall off."

Mr. Alcott shrugged. "Perhaps one of the other guests stopped by and dropped it."

"I wonder who," the woman said.

"It could have also been the groundskeeper who has forgotten it." Mr. Alcott turned to the man behind him. "Now that you've seen my Orangerie, how about we return indoors? I'm certain Murphy has had long enough of a refreshment break and is primed to play some more."

"Wonderful idea," the woman agreed. Willa let out a sigh, her tense muscles relaxing.

Once they had left, Willa and I clambered out from underneath the workbench. I brushed away a bit of dirt on Willa's cheekbone.

"We were almost caught. I am thankful that they did not stay longer."

Willa nodded, her face turning pensive. "I suppose there was not a need to hide. We could have just said we were taking a look at the trees. No one would have been the wiser."

I grabbed her hand. "Your cheeks were as bright as the apples we get at the market."

"And yours weren't?" Willa's brow rose.

I chuckled. "Never said that." I ran my thumb across the inside of her palm. "My whole body felt as if it was exuding heat. I—" I lowered my lashes.

"I feel the same." Willa turned her head and sighed. "I wanted to kiss you when we danced at the Farnsby's ball, but then Beth returned, and there was no longer a right time." Her gaze caught mine, green eyes piercing my soul. "Anne, I like you."

A lump formed in my throat, obstructing my windpipe. I swallowed, my eyes never leaving Willa's.

"I like you too."

<h1 style="text-align:center">14</h1>

<h1 style="text-align:center">The Lucky One</h1>

Returning to my bedroom at the rented house, I couldn't help but skip across the floorboards, limbs filled with frenetic energy. I kept thinking about Willa, and it made me shake with excitement.

She had kissed me.

Me.

I reached towards the doorknob, knowing that I would spend the rest of the night thinking about Willa as I lay in bed. How her lips pressed against mine, how she tasted. I would never look at an orange the same again.

"Anne."

"Hmm?" I dropped my hand and turned around. Beth stepped out of her bedroom, looking flustered.

What had she been doing? "I imagined you would be asleep by now. Did I wake you? I was trying to be quiet."

"You did not wake me." Beth rushed forward, enveloping

me in a hug. She heaved against me. I guessed something was on her mind, and she needed to feel the comfort of a friend.

"What is that for?" I tucked my chin in against her shoulder, tightening my arms around her. I hoped my question would prompt an answer from Beth, but she avoided the truth.

"I am just glad you've returned." Beth hesitated. "Now, tell me, how was your night?"

We entered my room, and I told her about sharing my first kiss with Willa. My excitement bubbled over as we crawled up onto the bed and brushed her hair. But I kept a close watch on Beth; I worried about her.

Beth had been downtrodden ever since she had found out that the man she had been seeing wasn't an Irish duke at all. Nevertheless, I did not think that her heartbreak over being deceived by the imposter was the only thing on her mind. I could not shake the feeling that something more was bothering Beth. Perhaps I could not coax it out of her. Perhaps I needed to be more direct.

I pursed my lips and poked Beth's chest. "And what about you? What are you going to do?"

Beth's lashes lowered, her gaze moving everywhere but towards me.

I hated seeing Beth distraught. At the beginning of the season, she had been so excited to meet new people and attend balls that it pained my heart to see her sulk. "Will you stop thinking about that man, whoever he is?" There was still time for her to enjoy the season. I wanted to see Beth with a smile.

"The Gentleman Thief." Beth's eyes widened, and she raised her hand to cover her mouth in shock.

Wait... Did she just say? "What?"

"Nothing. It's nothing." Red crept up Beth's face, and I realized she had blurted out the truth. She was not sleeping yet when I returned home because she had left the house.

I leaned back and crossed my arms. "No, it is not nothing. That is why you wanted a hug. You went to see him tonight, am I right?"

What had Beth been thinking? She could have run into so many problems, and no one would have been around to help. No one would have even known where she was.

My scowl deepened. "Is that why you stayed home to begin with? To sneak out and confront him? Where did you even find the man? He was not at the duke's estate."

Beth's face ashened as I barraged her with my list of questions. She looked at me, face scrunched up and sad. Her voice was low and dispirited. "I guessed that since he was escorting Mary Chapman at the musicale, he might be in attendance at another event where she was present."

As soon as Beth said the name Mary Chapman, I knew where she had gone. "The opening of the new warehouse on the docks. I read that in the papers." Had she really gone there at night? Beth's blank expression was enough of a confirmation. "You went there by yourself? Anything could have happened. What were you thinking?" I wanted to shake some sense into her.

"I found him," Beth said. "He was renting a room near the Thames. I knocked on his door and demanded he tell me who he was."

I did not know what to say. Beth might quite possibly be the luckiest person alive to return to her room in one piece.

I stood from my bed and reached for the pitcher of water on my dresser, pouring myself a glass.

"He told me his nom de guerre, the Gentleman Thief." Beth crossed her legs.

I took a sip of water and swallowed, taking a moment to consider. "You should report him to the Bow Street Runners."

"No." Beth's face turned purple in her haste to speak. "I will not. I cannot."

I set down my glass of water. "Why in heaven not?"

Beth unfurled her legs and stood as well. She paced around, letting out a weary chuckle. "It is funny. If I had only paid attention to the other people at the courthouse that day of William's hearing, I would have recognized him from the very start. It is strange to think we have crossed paths before London." She paused, seconds passing until she added, "He is a good person."

A good person? "The Gentleman Thief is a criminal. There are warrants out for his arrest." I grabbed Beth's arm. I wanted her to acknowledge how dangerous her outing had been. "You put yourself in a lot of danger tonight. Who knows what he might have done?"

A strange look crossed Beth's face as crimson crept up her neck. It reminded me of my face when I thought about Willa.

Beth and the fake duke had already kissed. Had she done more?

No.

"Did he? Are you?" I asked it gently, gauging her reaction.

Beth shook her head. "No."

I let out a sigh of relief. "Good." I wanted Beth to find

happiness with someone that could give her all the love she deserved.

"He kissed me, but that is all. We did not take things further." Beth chewed her lip.

I had to ask, though I already anticipated what Beth would say. "And you will not report him?"

"No." Beth's answer was firm, leaving no room for discussion. "Despite his lies, he is a good man."

Unbelievable.

I laughed. "Look at the two of us; one has fallen for a thief while the other needs to marry for money but loves someone she cannot marry."

Beth's gaze snapped towards me. "Love?"

I shrugged. There was no reason to deny it now. "I suppose I do."

"Willa is very lucky." Beth offered me a smile.

I considered myself the lucky one. If only I could find a way to stay by Willa's side.

***

The next day, what was supposed to be a fun outing to Gunter's Tea Shop for ice cream turned into a chase against the clock. Outside the sweets shop, John, Rose, Beth, and I ran into Mr. Devensies.

The solicitor was an acquaintance of John who had tracked down the Gentleman Thief. He told us all about the sting operation set up by the Bow Street Runners that would take place that evening at Covent Garden Theater.

I'd joined Beth as she hurried to search for the Gentleman

Thief to warn him of the danger, but he was nowhere to be found. We had no choice but to call over a cab and return to John and Rose. Beth would have to tell them the truth and persuade her brother to help her intercept the Gentleman Thief at the theater. I wondered if Willa could help.

When Beth and I exited the carriage, I turned to the driver. "Can you deliver a message for me?"

"I don't have time for messages; I need customers," the driver said, scratching his beard stubble with a meaty finger.

I frowned and pulled my reticule from my pocket. It weighed little in my hand but should still have enough coin to entice the driver. "I will pay you all the money I have on me." I took out the coins and held them out to him. "Please."

The driver huffed. He grabbed the coins and stared at the small stack of money in his hands. "That is not enough to cover what potential clients could pay. I am running a business, not a charity."

Beth jumped in, dropping more coins in his palm. "This should more than cover your day's wages." Her voice was frosty.

Weighing the coins, the man's lips turned up into a smirk. "Pleasure doing business with you ladies. Now, what's the message, and where's it going?"

I breathed. "Go to the Marquis of Bambreich's house and ask for Willa Balfour. Tell her that we need her help with the duke and to meet us as soon as she can, either at Beth's or, if it is later, at the Covent Garden Theater."

15

⚬⚬⚬

Time And Space

A large crowd gathered outside the Covent Garden The-ater, abuzz with excitement about the soon-to-be-performed play. John and Rose were busy purchasing tickets while Beth stood next to me, picking at the seam of her dress. Her head bobbed back and forth between watching both sides of the street and scanning the crowd for the face of the man she was trying to save.

I wondered if the carriage driver had delivered the mes-sage to Willa and if she would come.

"Do you think we'll find him?" Beth's voice was shaky as she looked at me with a worried expression.

I exhaled slowly; I did not want to add to Beth's worry. "We are all here to find him. We can only hope that we do so in time. Perhaps sneak him out through the crowd so he does not get spotted by the Bow Street Runners."

Beth had spotted the Bow Street Runners earlier, two

of them veering off into a side street. Most likely, there were multiple men posted all around the theater, observing every exit.

"Perhaps there is no need to worry, and he isn't even going to attend the theater this evening." Beth nodded as if to convince herself.

The wide double doors at the front of the theater swung open, and the crowd started moving single file into the foyer. The red carpet stretched out like a tongue beckoning guests into its belly.

John and Rose returned, tickets in hand. "Ready?" John said, handing Beth and me a ticket. But Willa had not yet arrived, and I could not leave her alone waiting in the street.

"You go ahead." I squeezed her arm. "Find Henry. I am going to wait for Willa and keep an eye out for him here. Perhaps he's running late, and I can intercept him."

Beth steeled her face and nodded. "All right. If you do find him...Please, take him to our home and make him wait for me there."

"I will."

Beth pulled me into a quick hug.

John pursed his lips and frowned. "Anne, be careful. Don't take any unnecessary risks. You are still under my guardianship, and I cannot let anything happen to you. Your brother would never forgive me."

I snorted. "You do not need to worry. I will be fine by myself. I doubt I will be alone for very long."

"All right, let's go." Beth grabbed hold of her brother and sister-in-law.

The three of them darted off into the theater while

I remained on the sidewalk, watching every carriage that passed me by. After some time, a black carriage halted in front of me. The door slammed open, and out popped a red head of hair.

"Did you find him?" Willa wasted no time, stepping out of the carriage. She handed the driver his fee before turning back to me. That's when I noticed that Willa did not come alone. Melinda exited the carriage after her.

"Well, did they?" Willa asked again, impatience flavoring her voice.

"No, I was waiting for you. Beth, John, and Rose are searching for him inside.

"Where do you want us to search?" Melinda turned to me after straightening her dress. The carriage driver urged on his horses and drove off.

"I'm not certain. Perhaps we should split and walk around the building?"

Shrill whistles reverberated across Covent Garden.

"We found 'im," a man could be heard shouting as more burst forth from their hiding places in the alcoves and shadowed corners around the theater, dressed in their signature black top hats and black button-down jackets.

My eyes widened, and I looked at Willa. "They found him, as in, they found Beth's Henry? What do we do now?"

The Bow Street Runners headed left around the building, filing towards the back of the theater. I sprinted after them, my heart pounding in my chest.

Beth would be heartbroken if Henry was caught.

I veered around the corner and skidded to a stop. In the distance, a blonde woman struggled against one of the constables near the back entrance of the theater, hands tied behind her back.

They caught Beth. I squeezed my hands into fists, nails digging into the skin of my palms. What was I to do now?

Beside Beth, Henry was putting up a fight with a second constable. The stocky Bow Street Runner wrangled Henry in front of him and shoved his head down.

Willa and Melinda caught up with me.

Willa's voice came out in jagged spurts as she regained her breath. "Is there anything we can do? We can't let them take her and Henry."

Melinda looked grim. "There is nothing I can do at the moment; Beth and Henry will need to find a way to escape from them on their own. If I want to get them, I will need some space between them and the constables."

"How? How can you get them?" Willa glanced towards Beth and Henry, a crease deepening between her brows.

"My bookshop. I'll transport them." Melinda's voice sounded clipped while she fished a necklace from behind her dress. She pointed at us. "I'll do my best to retrieve them. You two, go find John and Rose. We'll meet back up at the Eastons' rental."

Melinda disappeared before we could react. One second, she had been standing in front of us, and the next, she was gone.

Willa's face ashened, and her mouth popped open. "How—"

I was just as confused. I knew Melinda was magical, but to see a person disappear into thin air was not something you could know, let alone anticipate.

I shook my head and flashed Willa an apologetic smile.

"I don't know. But we should do as she said and find John and Rose."

Still wary, Willa nodded. She gripped her skirts and glanced around, the streets once again empty of Bow Street Runners. "To the entrance?"

"Yes."

We hurried back around the theater building until we reached the front. I turned to Willa with a relieved sigh, then pointed at the entrance. "At least we won't have to go searching."

Willa's gaze followed the direction of my pointing, where we both watched John stride out of the double doors with Rose in tow, both their brows knitted in worry. John's eyes widened when he spotted me, and his pace increased.

"Have you seen them? Do you know what happened?" John hardly breathed as his words tumbled out. His eyes darted between Willa and me as he waited for an answer.

Willa spoke first. "They were caught by the policemen but—"

"Caught?" John looked horrified. "Where did they go?"

Rose placed her hand on John's arm, stroking his bicep. "I know you're worried, but let them finish. Once we know everything, we can think of what to do next."

John glanced at his wife and nodded before turning his gaze back at us. "So?"

"They managed to break away," I continued. "Melinda said she would get Beth and Henry."

Willa nodded. "She disappeared right in front of us."

"Yes, and she told us to find you and meet back up at your home in Covent Garden."

Rose pursed her lips. "Melinda said that?"

John did not seem assured. "What if Melinda can't get them?"

Rose gripped her husband's hand. "It does us no good standing here. We should return home and hope Melinda will bring Beth and Henry back with her. We can come up with a different plan later."

The four of us returned to John's rental home, where we remained standing in the back garden as we waited for the return of Melinda, Beth, and Henry.

"We could hail you a cab to return home," Rose told Willa. "It is getting late. You do not have to stay here waiting with us."

Willa glanced at me, her beautiful eyes searching mine, then she shook her head. "No, I'd rather stay and wait. I...There's..." She swallowed as her chin dipped down. "I have got some questions."

Rose nodded, then turned to Tom, the stable master, and Estelle, who had been keeping Tom company as he took care of the horses for the evening. "You might see and hear some strange things this evening, Tom. If you have any questions, I am certain Estelle can answer them for you, but I hope you will keep what happens here a secret?"

Tom fidgeted with the hay in his hands while Estelle nudged his arm. "Yes, ma'am." He tipped his head at Rose.

"Thank you, Tom. I appreciate it."

Willa inched in closer to me. "How long do we have to wait?" Goosebumps sprinkled across her fair arms. I unwrapped my shawl and pulled it around her shoulders, earning a grateful smile. "Thank you." She'd said it so softly it was barely a whisper.

"We can take a seat?" I grabbed her hand and led her toward the stable. There were a few benches there we could use as we waited for the arrival of Melinda, Beth, and Henry. I pressed my arm around her chilled skin as we sank onto a bench while John lit a few lanterns to brighten up the ever-darkening sky.

As John started the flames in the last candle, there was a loud thud in the middle of the back garden. Willa gasped at the reappearance of Melinda, Beth, and Henry.

John turned around and dropped the kindling. "Beth?" He strode towards Beth and gripped both her shoulders. "Are you all right?"

I held Willa a bit tighter as we watched the scene unfold in front of us.

Beth stood as if in a daze, her eyes glancing around the garden, moving from John to Tom and Estelle to us and back to John. She nodded at her brother.

John scanned his sister for injury, then, once he ascertained that she was whole, turned to Henry with a dark expression. "What is the meaning of involving my sister in your danger-ous schemes?" John shoved his hand against Henry's chest. Henry remained passive as he was pushed back. I assumed he agreed that he was the one at fault for endangering Beth. "You are incredibly fortunate you managed to escape. If it had not been for Beth's pleading, we would not have troubled our-selves with your affairs." John's barbed words struck true.

Henry lowered his gaze in shame, but Beth was having

none of it. "Stop it." She pushed John's arm away, her face furious, and stepped in between him and Henry.

John shook his head at his sister. "You could have been arrested alongside that man. I think you have done enough for now. You saved the Gentleman Thief and can return home while he will be leaving for Ireland this very moment." John glared at Henry and motioned towards the stable master. "Ready the carriage, Tom."

Beth crossed her arms, her expression signaling war. I had never seen Beth this fierce. "John Easton, I will not leave Henry. If we leave, we leave together." She grabbed Henry's hand, squeezing it tight, and moved beside him. Her gaze never left John's face. "I will always be your sister, but I am old enough to make my own decisions. You listened to me earlier today, so please do so again... I love the man beside me." Beth's voice softened, and for a moment, she looked at Rose before returning her gaze to John. "And I am of a mind to stay with him forever." Beth hesitated for only a moment when a smile crept up her face, and she turned to Henry. "I know this is not traditional. But would you do me the honor of becoming my husband?"

Beth looked so happy when Henry agreed to marry her. After, even as she continued talking things out with her brother, there was a lightness to her words, a joyfulness permeating her entire being. I admired Beth's tenacity; no matter the cost, she chose to do what would make her happy. I so hoped she would be happy with Henry, even if I would miss having my friend near.

Willa gripped my hand. "You can always visit her in

Ireland. And perhaps, in due time, Beth and Henry will be free to visit Westbridge again?"

"I hope so," I told Willa as we moved towards Beth to say our goodbyes after Rose and John.

Melinda enveloped Beth in a hug. Beth's face almost disappeared behind Melinda's bouncy curls. "Good luck, Beth. This is not what I imagined, but I am glad you have found your happily ever after." She tightened her hug before scraping her throat. "Well, I shall leave you all to it. Good luck on your journey."

I moved in next. Despite feeling sad that I was saying goodbye to my best friend, I plastered a smile on my face and wrapped my arms around her. Beth sighed against me, and I pressed my face against her cheek. "Stay safe." I wasn't certain what else to say, so I punctuated my words with an even tighter hug.

"Visit me in Ireland?"

"I would not dare miss your wedding."

"You are always welcome, Anne. I hope we can still see each other regularly." Beth pressed her chin against my shoulder. "Perhaps together with Willa?" Her voice was filled with meaning.

"Perhaps." A smile tugged at my lips.

Willa said her goodbyes to Beth last, then we all followed Beth and Henry to the front of the building, where Tom and Estelle waited with the readied carriage.

John had kept his composure during goodbyes, but as soon as Beth's carriage vanished from view, he deflated. Rose noticed and hooked her arm around his. "How about we go inside and get some tea, hmm?"

John nodded. "Tea sounds like a good idea."

John and Rose returned indoors while Melinda, Willa, and I still stood out front.

Without a word, Melinda turned around and headed towards the side gate that led to the back garden. Before I could say anything, Willa stormed off after Melinda.

"Wait! I want some answers."

I hurried off after Willa, closing the side gate behind me only to find Melinda stopped and staring at Willa.

"How did you disappear?" Willa asked Melinda. "This is the first time I have seen you do anything out of the ordinary. I mean...I knew. Anne, Beth, and I have discussed the fact that you are from a different time. But to see it, to really see you disappear..." Willa shook her head. "It is confounding, to say the least. I can scarcely believe it is true."

Melinda inhaled, chest expanding. "I am a time traveler from the future. I own a magical bookshop, and I help people from one time meet their potential soulmate in another."

"You are truly from the future?" Willa froze. I wondered what was going through her mind before her eyes darted to me. "If you are here to help other people find love then who is your mission now? It can't be Beth." She chewed her lip, eyes darting to me. "Surely you do not mean to help Anne?"

Her hurt look sent a pang through my heart. Was she jealous?

Melinda sighed. "I can't be certain. All I know is that the bookshop sent me here for a reason, I still have to find out what that reason is. For a time, I was under the impression that I was meant to help Beth but I think it is clear that she managed to help herself." Melinda let out a chuckle.

I raised my brows. "Wait, I don't think I play a part in your time travel schemes. I have no need for a dalliance with someone from a different time."

Willa seemed to consider more thoughts because she pointed her finger at Melinda. "What about my father? I've watched both of you interact these past weeks. I have not seen him this spirited since before my mother passed away. Are you going to leave him and return to your own time? You would break his heart toying with his affections like this and disappearing without a trace."

"Willa, that has never been my intention."

"Then what is your intention? Are you going to stay?" Willa pursed her lips as her pale green eyes stared at Melinda.

"Yes." Melinda's answer was not much louder than a whisper. Then, straightening her posture, she repeated herself. "Yes."

While Willa gawked at Melinda, I took my chance to take her slackened hand and envelop it with mine.

"I haven't spoken to your father, but I have been considering getting an apprentice. At first, I was considering Beth. But... Well, she has happily run off to Ireland now, hasn't she? I suppose, if I want to stay here, there is another option."

Another option? I perked my ears, wondering where Melinda was headed.

"Perhaps you two would like to be my apprentices?"

"The both of us?" Willa pointed to herself and me.

"Yes, I could teach you the ropes, and then you both could decide on taking over the Magical Bookshop. It is a lot of responsibility and has its downsides, but you could travel time and space...together."

My heart pounded in my chest, and I was lost for words. Was this a real offer? Could that be the future for me and Willa? I could not even imagine what traveling through time entailed, but any kind of traveling together with Willa sounded like a dream come true.

But... What about my family? I had been distracted from my duties, too caught up in Willa to even think about suitors. But the very real possibility of the financial ruin of my family remained. Could I be selfish and accept an offer like this in favor of helping my family? What about assuring that my sister has a chance to marry for love instead of money? I felt torn.

Beside me, Willa beamed. "You can teach us? Anne and I get to travel and see different times and places?"

Melinda nodded. "What do you both think?"

"Yes, yes. I would love to," Willa chirped. "Anne?"

How could I decline an offer to travel and learn about time travel with Willa? I did not have to make a final decision just yet. Perhaps things might change in the future, and I could choose what I wanted to do. My family's situation was dire, but the debt had not been called in yet.

"Yes." I squeezed Willa's hand and grinned.

16

Necklaces

Willa fidgeted beside me, shifting her legs as we waited for Melinda's arrival. She'd been nervously pacing the foyer, but I managed to get her seated on the tufted foot bench, which pressed against the wall on the side of the grand staircase.

"What do you think it feels like?" Willa glanced at me; her mouth puckered as she thought.

"Does what feel like?"

"Time travel. Do you think it hurts? Where do our bodies go?"

"I am not inclined to think it would hurt. Melinda has never appeared to be in pain, and when Beth and Henry returned, they did not seem to be in pain either—confused, for certain, but not in pain."

Willa nodded. "I suppose I am more nervous about the unknown. I wish the experience would be over so I can know what to expect next time." Her brows raised slightly. "You do not appear nervous in the least."

I snorted. "Then I am doing an admirable job of hiding it." My insides had been in turmoil all morning, churning and spinning at the thought of leaving my own time. The only thought that helped settle my nerves was the knowledge that it wouldn't merely be me; I would have Willa by my side.

Lips quivering into a smile, Willa shook her head. "Still, I envy your composure." She slid her hand over, lacing her fingers with mine. "I am glad we are in this together."

"Me too," I said as she leaned in against me.

It had been nearly a week since our kiss at Mr. Alcott's Orangerie, and I still felt the tension between us. So many things had happened in between that we had not had the chance to discuss any of it. All I knew was that her presence made my heart race and that every moment she wasn't by my side, I found myself thinking of her. I would eat tarts made by John's hired cook and think how much Willa would enjoy the flavor or read a funny anecdote in the paper and regret not being able to share it.

Having Willa beside me felt... right.

A knock on the door shook me from my ruminations.

Willa straightened and pulled her hand from my grasp. "That should be Melinda." She stood and opened the door, revealing Melinda wearing a bright smile.

"Ready, ladies?" she said, striding in, full of energy. Melinda was still wearing skirts of a kind, but I did not recognize them to be anything like the fashion I was used to. I wondered if she had worn different clothing from usual on purpose. "Is your father around?"

Willa shook her head. "He retreated to his study. However, we should hurry; I do not want him to catch us and start asking questions."

"Right, right. Let's head outside then." Melinda motioned to the back.

Why did she always leave from the garden? Was being outside a requirement to travel? "We can't leave from here?" I stood from the bench, brushing the creases from my dress.

"No." Melinda flashed another smile. "But it is better to do it away from prying eyes, plus there's less furniture to contend with." Melinda's eyes crinkled, and she headed into the hallway. "This one time, I appeared in a small room, completely dark; I took one step and tumbled over some kind of stool, landing flat on my face. The noise alerted the entire house."

Willa and I followed her.

Melinda glanced back with a smile. "That was the last time I appeared indoors. I was aiming for my client's bedroom but had gotten the building's layout wrong." Pausing for a moment, she continued. "The fastest path to the garden is through the first door on our left, correct?"

"The parlor, yes. It has an exit to the side garden," Willa said.

Without missing a beat, Melinda opened the door and swept into the sitting room, where the chairs and couches sat invitingly in the same shimmering velvet I remembered from my previous visit.

"Come along then; I am sure you both are ready to get things started." She stopped in the middle of the room, eyeing the wainscotted walls for the exit door. "Now where..."

Willa hurried to her right, where she swung open a door that had blended in well with the dark drapery.

"Perfect," Melinda muttered as she swept past Willa and moved outside.

Willa flashed me a nervous smile before exiting as well.

Once I joined them in the garden, Melinda fetched a pouch from a pocket in her skirt.

"Now, I've prepared some things for you. I am already wearing my necklace..." With her left hand, she pulled forward a simple necklace that hung around her neck.

The last time Melinda used the necklace, I was too confused and worried about Beth and Henry to pay attention. But now, I could finally take a good look. The shape of the stone was irregular and faintly iridescent; it almost pulsated the way its color shifted between emerald and jade and a shade even darker.

The color reminded me of the foliage on the trees that backed up to my family's property. I loved taking a walk and wandering through the thick of it on my own. Surrounded by those tall, dark trees covered in lichen, my nose filled with that specific earthy scent, which made me feel calm and soothed.

Those woods had especially been a refuge after my father's passing when I was too angry to remain indoors. I blamed my father for his gambling. I blamed Randolph. I even blamed my mother for not knowing of my father's addiction and unwittingly forcing me to step up for my family. But I could not share any of that with them. What was the point? My words would do nothing to solve the problems at hand; I would only be hurting them.

So I walked.

"Anne, are you ready?" Willa's face lit up with excitement.

Melinda opened the pouch and took out two more necklaces. "These are for you," she said, handing them to us. "They are the same as mine. I promise that I will answer any questions and explain how they work when we arrive. Now, I want you to put them around your neck but be careful not to touch the stone just yet, okay?"

Willa nodded gravely as she pulled the leather cord around her face, fishing out her thick red hair from underneath with a sweep of her hand. I followed suit and gingerly grasped the cord by its sides, making sure that none of my fingers neared the stone.

"Good, good." Melinda nodded, a mischievous smile plastered on her face. "The next part will be easy. I am going to take you to my magical bookshop so I want you both to hold on to me and think of where I am taking you."

"What about the necklace?" I glanced down at the stone pressing against my clavicle. "Do we need to do anything with that?"

Melinda's smile widened. "Not this time. Today you are traveling with me. However, I will tell you more once we are in my bookshop. Willa, Anne, can you grab hold of my right arm?"

Melinda returned the empty pouch to her skirt pocket and then held out her arm for us. Willa grabbed Melinda's hand, her whitening knuckles telling me that she was squeezing it tight. I took a firm grip on her forearm.

"Just stay calm while I reach for my necklace; the traveling itself takes less than a second. You won't even notice you have left."

"All right," Willa squeaked.

Melinda moved her left hand towards the stone, which was glowing brighter.

"Ready, set..."

"Willa," a man's voice said from the doorway.

"Go."

I caught a last glimpse of Willa's father, the Marquis of Bambreich, before my vision blurred.

Willa's face drained of color while my ribcage squeezed inward; bile flooded my mouth, making it hard to breathe. Flecks of darkness dotted my vision. Then the world around me turned black.

With a thud, we landed. My breath returned as I dropped Melinda's arm and keeled forward, heaving, my knees dented against a hardwood floor. It took a few deep breaths before I managed to tip my head up and take a look at my surroundings. Willa was still standing, albeit a bit flustered, while Melinda did not seem bothered by the sensations that I felt.

"It will pass," Melinda said, holding out her hand. "The first time tends to be the worst, and everyone reacts differently. I reckon you are seasick as well?" She nodded knowingly.

I grasped her hand and pulled myself back to standing. "I would not know; I haven't had a chance to test it—boats."

"Was that my father?" Willa said. Her brows had knitted together, and her lips were pale as she chewed her lower lip. "Do you think he... you know."

"Saw?" Melinda pursed her lips in sympathy. "Yes, I would assume that he saw us disappear into thin air."

I stifled a snort. Melinda had answered so bluntly, it physically stunned Willa.

Willa's face took on a look of horror. "Perhaps he was looking in a different direction?"

"As he was calling your name?" Melinda shook her head. "No, I think we'll have to give him an explanation when we return. I doubt that he has come up with a plausible theory for our disappearance."

"Witchcraft," I said. My stomach was starting to settle, though a sour taste remained.

"Don't tease." Willa rolled her eyes. "I did not want to worry him, and now we are here while he is assuredly wondering what happened to us." She let out a harsh puff of breath and craned her neck as she glanced around.

Brushing Willa's sleeve, I slipped my hand around hers. "I know; I am sorry, Willa. But there is nothing we can do about it now. We have to make the most of Melinda's lesson. We'll find out about your father's thoughts when we return."

"Anne is right. And it would be a waste to return to this moment." Melinda spoke with a soothing voice and offered a thoughtful expression. "Come, I'll put the kettle on, then we can settle our nerves, and"—she shot me a quick nod—"soothe your stomach a bit."

I perked up. "There's a kitchen?"

So far, all I'd noticed were the heavy wooden bookcases, creating narrow aisles to wander through. And in the back, a short staircase led to a loft area with even more books lining the wall.

I took a moment to appreciate my surroundings. With the notion of time travel fresh in my mind, I hadn't been certain of what to expect. But now that I stood here, it was recognizable as a bookstore. At first glance, things did not seem that different from bookstores in Westbridge or London. Although... Now that I paid more attention, it seemed to me that the lighting was different, harsher.

I glanced up at the ceiling and marveled at the illuminated spheres dotting the white surface. How did they work? It wasn't fire, of that I was certain.

Melinda must have caught my perplexed face because she pointed at the lights. "Electricity."

"Electricity?" I'd heard of electricity before, but all it brought to mind was the strange device I had seen at an exhibition in London. A strange contraption that consisted of a glass cylinder that could be turned fast by a wooden handle to create friction. Then the demonstrating gentleman would use one of the wire-attached sticks of some sort to send a shock into a person's limb. I had been appalled at the idea of letting anyone near me with that wooden stick. To think that same power was illuminating the ceiling here.

"I can show you both more," Melinda said. "My kitchen is also powered by electricity." She waved her hand and turned to the left.

Willa and I followed Melinda, brushing past the sales counter topped with what looked like some kind of cash register, though smoother than I was used to and painted uniformly gray.

I'd been too focused on other things that I had failed to notice the door behind the counter. Melinda opened it and swept inside.

"Welcome to my home of the last few decades," she said, waving her arms around the cramped space.

Against the wall, on the left, there was a bit of counter space on either side of the stove, a kettle sitting atop it. Melinda picked out a box from the storage space above.

"I'm thinking peppermint," she said, sniffing the vividly colored thin squares. "That'll be just the thing to set a stomach at ease." She lifted the kettle and twirled it side to side, sloshing the liquid inside. Agreeing with the volume inside, she nodded to herself and lit the stove. I watched as one of the burners made a clicking noise, then sparked and finally produced a bluish flame. Melinda glanced back once she'd set down the kettle. "Go on and have a seat, the both of you." She pointed to a small cloth-draped table and set of chairs. The edge of the cloth was lined in small daisies.

Dazed with the onslaught of new information, I took a seat at the table. Willa remained equally silent as she sat across from me.

Melinda's living quarters were smaller than I was used to, only the kitchen area and, from what I could see through the open door behind me, a small bedroom. There was another door that was closed, which I presumed to be the bathroom.

I bit my lip and watched Melinda at the stove. There were so many questions racing through my mind that they stalled and rendered me mute. Willa's eyes were bright as she ogled the room, shooting glances at me every few moments.

A few minutes later, Melinda ambled over, carrying two steaming cups of tea, the fresh scent of peppermint wafting towards us.

Willa accepted her cup of tea, wrapping her elegant hands

around the porcelain. "How does it work?" she said, breaking the silence.

"The bookshop is powered by a magical stone." Melinda returned with a cup of her own.

I pulled out my new necklace by the string. "The same as this?" I looked down my nose to the green stone resting against my clavicle.

"One and the same." Melinda blew on the hot liquid in her hand. "You can think of me as the facilitator and custodian of the bookshop, but what is actually in charge is the stone. In fact, it is the foundation of this entire place."

"In charge of doing what?"

"Bringing potential soulmates together regardless of time and space."

Willa interjected with a frown, "But how?"

"Even I am not a hundred percent certain. This bookshop has existed for much longer than I have been alive, and I am not the first owner, nor am I the only custodian. There are more of us out there."

My mouth slackened. "More? There are more time travelers?" Many theories had crossed my mind, but never once had I considered there were more people like Melinda out there.

Melinda nodded and sipped her tea. "Surely you did not think I was in charge of all time travel across the globe and all centuries? No, my bookshop seems to only travel back to your time. I can hop distances like I did when I rescued Beth and Henry, but other than that, it is a direct line from your time to my time."

Willa's eyes moved sideways, and an intense expression painted on her face as she pursed her lips in rumination. "So

Anne and I would be traveling the same timeline if we took care of the bookshop?"

"Yes."

Once we drained our cups, Melinda took us on a tour, showing us all the nooks and crannies of the bookshop. Willa and I witnessed everything in wonderment until more than two hours had passed, and Melinda stopped her explanations.

"I think I've talked enough for one day. We should head back to the manor and see how your father is." Melinda smiled at me. "Don't worry, Anne, you should find the second time a bit more manageable, and it will get easier in time. Although, traveling does take a toll no matter what. You may find yourself unusually fatigued tonight. Both of you should take care to eat a good, full meal."

Willa offered a firm nod.

I considered for a moment before looking up at Melinda. "What's the toll?"

"It takes a lot of energy to travel. Doing too much too often will deplete your body's resources and make you feel weak and tired. That's why you need to make sure to eat enough food and get enough rest, or you might end up stuck, unable to travel, for an indeterminate amount of time."

"Has that happened to you?"

Melinda smiled and shook her head. "No, but my mentor, the previous bookshop owner, has told me about the time it happened to her." She chuckled at our impressed faces. "Now, like we did the first time, let's all hold each other's arms and think of the garden outside Bambreich Manor."

17

A Lifetime

The sun had sunken lower in the sky, indicating to me that a similar amount of time had passed since our departure as we had spent at the bookshop. My stomach still roiled, but I remained upright, which was an improvement over my first traveling attempt.

Willa was the first to let go of Melinda's arm as well as my hand, spinning around to face her father, but there was no sign of the marquis outside.

"It has been hours," I told her. "He's probably gone inside."

Willa pursed her lips. "I imagined him waiting for us here, fuming and pacing as he wondered what had happened to us." Her green eyes met mine. "Is it cowardly to want to flee to my bedroom and avoid a confrontation?" Her lip lifted into a smile as she waited for my answer.

I shook my head. "Not at all. If it had been my brother or mother, I probably would have had the same thought. But postponing a conversation because you are worried about the other person's reaction has never helped resolve a situation. It might only make it worse."

Willa let out a deep sigh, her shoulders stiffening as she steeled herself for what was to come. "Let's find my father then. You'll stick by my side, right?"

"Of course." I flashed Willa an assuring smile. Leaving her while she was nervous about the conversation with her father would have never crossed my mind.

Melinda nodded and tucked a few flyaway curls behind her right ear. "We'll all go in. Your father deserves an explanation from me."

Usually, Melinda moved through the world without caring what anybody thought of her. But to my surprise, I detected a hint of apprehension this time. She must care for the marquis and worry about his opinion of her.

Melinda curled her right arm around Willa's shoulders. "It'll be all right."

We did not need to go far; as soon as we entered the back of the mansion, I heard the scuffling of feet and then the swing of a door. The marquis darted out of the sitting room, his face at first worried, but then—once he'd ascertained our wellbeing—the worry lines on his face deepened into a disagreeable scowl. He stepped forward and straightened; the creases in his jacket from sitting remained. They must have set after hours of waiting.

"What happened?" he asked, gaze sweeping over us. "It's been hours since you..." The marquis hesitated, more than likely worried he would seem like a madman if he confessed what he'd seen.

"Disappeared?" A small smirk appeared on Melinda's face.

The marquis' eyes narrowed. "I came to find you and heard noises outside. Then one moment there you all were, and the next," he swallowed, "the next you were all gone. Like smoke. I need some answers."

Willa lifted her chin and confronted her father. "Papa, Melinda showed us how to travel through time. She's offered to teach us how to do it ourselves."

"Time travel?" The marquis' face reddened, his gaze flitting between Melinda and his daughter. "I don't know how that is even possible, but no daughter of mine is going to risk doing things we cannot understand." He grabbed Willa's wrist. "You are coming with me. You will go to your room and stay there until I say otherwise."

"I will not." Willa pulled against her father's grip. "This is my choice."

The marquis' voice boomed in anger. "You are my child, and you will listen to me. I had planned to secure a good match for you and keep you safe."

"Keep me trapped," Willa shot back. "I am not a porcelain doll. I will not break."

"Do not speak to me like you know what the world is like because you do not, I assure you."

"Francis..." Melinda's voice rang out.

The marquis shook his head and gripped Willa's arm tighter. "You do not interrupt. We will have words later."

"Papa, let go." Willa's face had turned ashen, except for patches of scarlet creeping up her cheeks. Her eyes watered as she stared at her father, who was still pulling at her arm. I could see the grip of his fingers leaving white indents on her arm. The small tremble of her lips made my heart squeeze in anguish.

"Stop." I grabbed the marquis' hand and tugged Willa's arm free before wrapping Willa into my embrace. A few tears had spilled over, wetting her cheek, which she pressed against my shoulder.

The marquis staggered backward, a flash of shock passing over his face, before he looked at his daughter. Some undefinable emotion warred within him—shame or regret, perhaps? His gaze dropped to the marks on her forearm, which she tenderly touched with her fingers.

"Francis," Melinda said again. She reached out to him and touched his shoulder. "I know this is a lot of new information. The idea is frightening; I get it. But isn't Willa allowed to make her own choices?"

Willa was still pressed against me, her head resting on my shoulder. I kept my arm tightened around her, thumb brushing her skin in comforting strokes.

The marquis glanced at his feet, his shoulders slumping. His voice was difficult to discern. "I am sorry."

"What?" Willa's lashes fluttered as she opened her eyes, and she brushed the tears on her cheek away with her palm.

"I am sorry," the marquis repeated, louder this time. He lifted his chin, brows softening. The angry red hue of his face had seeped away, and he wrung his hands while shooting a hesitant glance at Melinda. "I never wanted to hurt you, Willa. You are the best thing that ever happened to me, the spitting image of your mother." He shook his head and let out a soft sigh. "All I wanted was to keep you safe and secure. To be certain that you would be provided for after my passing."

The marquis' eyes turned to me; I felt his judgment as a certain understanding appeared in his gaze. He nodded with a regretful smile.

"Papa." Willa straightened and opened her mouth to say more, but the marquis shook his head.

"I know what you are going to say. I'm not that old yet; I have many years left to live. And you are right, but your mother's sudden passing reminded me how quickly things may change. We can never know when it is our time to leave this earth, and the thought of you, alone, is unbearable." The marquis' chest rose and fell as he took a deep breath. "You are so much like her; headstrong, smart, funny. Sometimes I wish you would listen to me a bit more, but I should have never tried to force my will upon you. Your mother would have wanted you to make your own decisions. She loved you so much. We both love you so much."

I let go of Willa as she burst forward and hugged her father, tears now streaming down her freckled cheeks. He kissed the top of her head and brushed back her hair with his hands as she pressed her face against his chest.

"I love you too, Papa."

Once the two finished hugging, the marquis turned to Melinda. "Is it safe?"

"Yes."

"Will I be able to see my daughter often?"

Melinda nodded. "She can come to visit you—us—as often as she'd like."

Satisfied with Melinda's answers, the marquis turned to me. His green eyes, so like his daughter, pierced me. "Will you stay by her side?"

The question, while simple, felt weighted with unexpressed meaning. Willa's father had seen our interaction and confirmed our feelings for each other went beyond friendship. Would I stay by Willa's side?

My heart leaped at the thought of spending every day with her, traveling time together and seeing the world. More than anything, I wanted to learn everything there was to know about Willa, count every freckle on her skin, and hear her every thought. I wanted a lifetime together. But I still had my family to consider. All I could hope for was that Randolph managed to find a way out of the debt so I could be free to choose my own life.

Then...

Then I would stay by her side.

"I will," I said, my voice hoarse with emotion.

The marquis smiled. "Then you take good care of my daughter."

18

Anywhere

"Are you certain we've traveled through time?" My stomach twinged, unsettled by the change of location, the only evidence I had that I had left. I wondered when I wouldn't feel nauseated anymore; Willa appeared to have no ill effects.

Melinda had told Willa and me that we would be traveling to the future, but my first glimpse of the future looked an awful lot like the same streets back home. I recognized our location, a street only a block away from Bambreich Manor lined with a row of upscale homes often for let during the London Season.

The wind whipped softly around my face, fanning my hair back. I walked forward, my foot stepping onto the road.

Wait...

I glanced down at the grayish material covering the street; a pair of bright yellow stripes lined the road, and another stripe in white lined the middle. Then I began to notice other differences.

The air smelled clean, cleaner than I had ever encountered in London. Usually, the city had a rather strong scent of horse manure from carriages, sewage, and other types of rubbish and waste. It was why most of the lords and ladies returned to the countryside during the summer months when the sweltering heat turned the streets into a malodorous breeding ground of putrefaction.

On the other side of the road, a few metallic contraptions were leaning against the wall of a house. They reminded me of a hobby horse. Although, these versions looked much easier to ride. My brother had once had the chance to try one of these velocipedes at an acquaintance's estate. Later, he had said that he much prefered traveling by horse over the shaky bumpy ride on that two-wheeled contraption.

"Anne!" Willa screamed my name.

I lurched around to see a horseless carriage with two lights speeding towards me. Before I could move, a hand gripped the back collar of my dress and pulled me back onto the stoop. A loud horn sounded from the carriage as it sped past. Willa's arms pulled around me, her hands trembling. I let out a puff of air, my breathing returning.

"You need to watch out," Willa said. "That...thing could have hit you."

I glanced back at her, barely able to move within her tight embrace. "I promise."

Finally, Willa let go of me, her hands dropping to her side. I straightened my skirts, trying to compose myself.

"And that was a car," Melinda said. She furrowed her brows and tipped her head at me. "Are you all right?"

I nodded and swallowed, checking back to see how far from the road I was standing and moving even further away.

Melinda snorted. "So, to answer your question, yes, we have traveled through time. About two hundred years."

"Two hundred years?" Willa let out an awed chuckle, her head craning around. "And all of these houses still exist? What else is the same? Is my home still here? Can we check?"

A man whistled, followed by chuckles from his fellow pedestrians strolling down the sidewalk. Removing his thumb and pointer finger from his mouth, he said, "Bit early for the ren fair, innit?"

Renfair? The word didn't mean anything to me, so I shrugged and looked at Melinda.

"Never too early to dress up," Melinda said with a quick smirk.

The whistler nodded, tipping his head to Melinda and stuffing his hands in the pockets of his trousers. His voice took on an exaggerated cadence. "Very true, my lady." Then chuckled as he continued on his way. The other men ogled us for a bit but soon passed out of view as well when they turned onto another street.

Melinda shook her head, curls bobbing, then turned to Willa. "We can go to Bambreich Manor. We have plenty of time to do some sightseeing." Melinda tapped her chin and turned her attention to me. "You did tell John and Rose to meet us this evening at Willa's home, right?"

I grinned. "Rose was elated about the prospect of food from her time. I am certain they will be ready and waiting for us with the marquis whenever we return." I thought for a moment, trying to remember the words Rose had spewed out in her excitement. "Rose said something about fast...food?"

"Ah, yes." Melinda smiled and nodded. "That would be impossible to find in your time. I wonder what we should get; pizza, burgers, Indian takeout, fish fry, Chinese." She sighed. "There are so many choices."

"One of everything?" Willa's brows raised as she teased Melinda.

"That would be a lot of food." Melinda laughed. "I'm certain you'll have more opportunities to bring back other kinds of food." She brushed her hair off her forehead. "Well, you wanted to see your home, right?"

Willa grinned and bobbed her head. "Yes, let's go." She grabbed my hand, and together we headed toward the end of the block, followed by Melinda.

It took us about fifteen minutes to walk to Bambreich Manor.

"It's still here," Willa said, perking up her head. "The gate is gone, but other than that, it looks the same."

I nodded, our hands swinging in tandem as we crossed the road. This time, I made certain there were no vehicles headed in our direction. The stately mansion stood proudly before us, the stone still colored in the same off-white paint.

"Those are new." I pointed at the lights mounted at the foundation surrounding the building, illuminating the stonework.

Willa worried her lip, glancing at me in question. "Do you think I could check? It's all so strange; I suppose I would like to see if it—"

"If someone else really lives there now?"

Willa nodded to me, then glanced back at Melinda.

Melinda heard what Willa said. "Be careful with what you say but go ahead; there's no harm in checking."

Willa kept a grip on my hand, and together we walked up the driveway to the stone columns surrounding the entrance. I noticed a round, blue plaque attached to the wall on the right side of the door. *Heritage Property*, it read, and underneath that were the words, *Home of the Duke of Bambreich*.

"They commemorated your family," I said.

Willa gazed at the plaque, a small frown between her brows. She leaned forward and used the brass knocker to announce our arrival.

A slender man of about thirty to forty years opened one side of the double doors. His light brown hair was neatly combed over, and he was dressed in a simple blue shirt and a pair of jeans. I remembered that fabric from Melinda showing us part of her wardrobe.

"Can I help you?" he said. "I'm afraid we don't do walk-in tours; if you'd like one, you would have to make an appointment in advance."

Willa was stunned. She stared at the man in silence.

The man shuffled his feet, half of his body still hidden behind the wooden door. "I can get you a business card. You can just call the number there. We do tours Tuesday through Sunday from ten to six. They last about an hour, though you are welcome to stay a bit longer to walk around and browse our collection of memorabilia and visit our small gift shop before the next group."

I smiled at the man. "Are you certain we can't take a tour

today?" I pointed at Willa and Melinda. "My friends and I have traveled quite far to visit Bambreich Manor, and we have to leave this afternoon. We would be ever so grateful, sir."

The man hesitated, taking in our dresses and our pleading faces. He sighed and shook his head, flashing a reluctant smile. "Fine, we've got about an hour before the first tour group arrives, so I suppose I can show you three around. A shorter tour than usual, mind you." He opened the door wider to let us in. "Call me George."

"Thank you, George," I told the tour guide.

True to his word, we spent about forty-five minutes following him around Bambreich Manor. He told us about previous residents and notable guests that had stayed there over the centuries. It was strange to hear this man spout facts and information about Willa and her family and her home as if it was ancient history when for us, it had been only hours ago.

"We are in the future," Willa said when we stepped out of the manor.

"Yes, there's no doubt about it."

"Come," Melinda said. "It is nearly lunchtime, and I am certain you both could use some food." She placed her arm behind Willa's back and led us down the driveway back to the street. "Let me make a suggestion."

"What?" I glanced up at Melinda.

A smile formed on her lips. "It might be nice to spend some time together, just the two of you. How about I go run some errands while you have lunch without me?"

"But what about you? Don't you need to eat something?"

Melinda shook her head. "Don't worry about me; I'll find something. Besides, I'd like to shop around for a bit and find a gift or something for Francis. Let us find a restaurant for you, and then I'll meet back up with you there in a couple of hours. Sound good?"

"All right," Willa said.

"Oh, before I forget." Melinda fetched a purse from her skirt pocket. "You'll need some spending money." She pulled out a few rectangular papers with the face of a lady in varying hues of blue, orange, purple, and red. "This should be more than sufficient," she said, stuffing them into my hands. "The values are printed on them, so it should not be too difficult to figure out. Menus have prices listed on them."

I nodded and added the paper currency to my small purse.

We had walked about three blocks when we spotted a restaurant, large tan window awnings covering a patio section and artificial golden light spilling out of windows that took up nearly the entire side of the building. Many people were dining inside and out, but peering inside, I noticed there were still a few open tables available.

"Look good?" Melinda said.

I glanced at Willa, who offered me a bright smile and wasted no time nodding to Melinda.

"Perfect, I will see you both in a couple of hours then."

"Wait, what if we are finished early?" I glanced around the area.

"There are plenty of shops so do some sightseeing. Just check back at this location for my arrival."

Melinda walked away, and Willa and I entered the dining facility together. A small bell rang above as the door closed behind us with a thud. A waiter dressed in all black shuffled over and welcomed us.

He took two menus from a nearby stand and propped them underneath his arm. The inside of the bistro was warm, with a square-shaped bar lining the kitchen and smaller wooden tables placed throughout the establishment, illuminated by the fans hanging from recessed embossed ceilings.

"Inside or outside?" the waiter asked.

"Inside, please." I flashed the waiter a pleasant smile.

He nodded and motioned to the back. "This way, please."

Willa glanced at me while we followed the waiter to a cozy corner, a shy smile playing on her lips that rivaled my expression.

Was this a date?

Was I truly on a date with Willa?

My heart bounced in my chest; I felt giddier than usual. Rose had mentioned dates before and said it was something people did in her own time. But I had never been on one; every meeting between eligible companions was always supervised and scheduled. It left little room for exploration and spontaneity. This led me to my next question…

What did someone speak about on a date?

The waiter paused for us to take our seats, then handed us our menus.

"Anything to start your meal? What about any drinks?"

I gawked at the smooth multi-papered menu in my hands. "Umm—"

"Perhaps some water?" Willa's clear voice interrupted my jumbled thoughts.

I nodded. "Yes." I turned to the waiter. "I think we need a moment to decide."

The waiter scribbled on a paper pad he pulled from a

pocket on his black apron. "I'll be right back with those and give you a few more minutes to review the menu."

Willa flipped a page. "There are so many options, and I hardly know what any of them mean. "Gyoza? Ceviche? Oh, wait, I know this one." She chuckled and pointed at a meal towards the bottom of the second page. "Beef bourguignon."

"Let's try something different. We can read the descriptions and share a few plates."

Willa's eyes sparkled as she met mine. "That's a splendid idea."

Twenty minutes later, a veritable feast lay spread out in front of us. We had chosen five kinds of appetizers to share as well as two glasses of the house wine, a robust red poured into massive globes nearly the size of my head.

"The gyoza was a great choice," Willa said between bites. She'd popped one of the meat-filled dough creations into her mouth with a bit of the accompanying spicy sauce and now licked the corners of her lips.

I swirled my glass and took a sip of wine. "The food is delicious." I did not know why I was so nervous about a date with Willa; her presence made everything better. I loved hearing her gasps of excitement when she tried new foods or seeing her red curls bouncing as she moved her hands animatedly while she told a story.

She was wonderful.

"Here, try this." Willa reached forward, one hand supporting a spoon loaded with shrimp while she cupped the other underneath to protect the table from spills.

I scooted forward and closed my mouth around the spoon, a burst of citrus and sweetness from the shrimp exploding on my taste buds. "Mmm, I'll end up spoiled for the food back home." I flashed Willa a teasing smile.

Willa chuckled as she leaned back again. She laid down the spoon and brushed back a few wisps of her hair before reaching towards my side of the table and grabbing my hand. "I am glad to experience this with you." Her face turned serious, and she squeezed my palm. "There is no one else I would rather be with right here and now."

Willa's face glowed in the golden light from the chandeliers, a charming blush affixed to her freckle-covered cheeks. My breath hitched, and I wondered how I could have gotten fortunate enough for her to return my affection.

"I would be with you anywhere."

19

❦

Fast Food

Our date had ended much too soon. However, Willa and I were both in high spirits as we returned to Bambreich Manor, especially with the surprise we had picked up in London.

"Anne and Willa, you're back." A wide smile lit up Rose's face as we strolled up to where she was standing in the marquis' front garden. "I was just taking a breath of fresh air." Rose patted the growing bump on her belly. "This baby decided it did not like the air indoors. I hope these bouts of nausea will soon pass." She crooked her head, glancing at what I was clutching in my left hand. "What's that?"

I thrust my hand behind my back, hiding the brown paper bag from her piercing gaze. "It is a surprise from Willa and myself. I promise you will find out soon enough."

Rose sniffed the air and smirked while nodding. "I am certain the others will be surprised... Well, let's get you both inside. Willa, your father has been most anxious for your return." She glanced back at me as she moved to the front door. "Is Melinda not coming?"

"She will be here in a moment. There was something she wanted to put together for the marquis."

Rose opened the door for us. "Oh good, I think the marquis was not only worried about his daughter." She crooked her brow at Willa. "But don't tell him I said any of that."

I kept the paper bag hidden behind my back, letting Rose lead us to the dining room. John and the marquis were chatting but ceased the moment the marquis spied us.

The Duke of Bambreich shot up, scraping back his chair. "Willa, Anne, you have returned. How was your journey?" His voice had a hint of urgency. His gaze flashed to a spot behind us. I ventured he was looking for Melinda.

Willa strode forward, crossing the distance between her and her father. "Papa, it was wonderful. You would not believe the things I saw and learned today." She clutched the marquis' hands. "However, I shall tell you all about it later. Right now, I have something for you to try."

Willa smiled so brightly back at me, it sent tremors through my heart. I returned the smile, then whipped the paper bag out from behind my back and held it up for every-one to see.

"I hope you are all hungry." I opened the bag and took out multiple wrapped items as well as paper boxes and placed them in the middle of the table.

Willa joined me and helped hand out the different items. "These are called burgers and fries. They are very popular in the future, right?" Willa looked to Rose for confirmation.

"That is right." Rose bobbed her head.

Once everyone had their food, Willa and I sat down. I unwrapped my burger, revealing the round flat bread topped with sesame seeds.

"They're made of minced meat, cheese, and vegetables, all sandwiched between two pieces of bread," I said aloud. I figured the marquis needed an explanation since he was turning the burger over in his hands as if he was examining something offensive. A mixture of curiosity and apprehension warred on his face.

"No utensils?" The marquis sounded affronted, as if we had made an error in propriety.

Willa laughed. "Papa, try it for me? It is supposed to be eaten with your hands. See, like this." She lifted the burger to her face, taking a bite.

Rose joined in and took a massive bite of hers, a swipe of red sauce lingering on her upper lip. "You try it too." She nudged her husband, John, urging him to take a bite. Rose swallowed another mouthful and sighed. "I've missed burgers... and fries...and vanilla shakes to dip the fries in." Rose opened one of the cardboard boxes and picked out a long, yellow slice of fried potato. She grinned widely as she gazed at Willa and me. "Thank you for surprising us with this."

"I am glad you like it," I told her.

Beside her, John groaned as he took a bite of the savory meat. "Mmm, this is delicious."

I was still quite full from lunch, but I still reached for one of the potato slices, their salt covering sticking to my fingertips. I savored the fry, then licked the tips of my fingers clean.

Willa leaned towards me. "This is very tasty, though it does not rival the food we ate earlier."

I glimpsed at Willa's face and spotted a smear of yellow beside her lips. "Are you certain?" I laughed and reached out my hand, swiping the sauce away with my pointer finger. "It seems you like it enough to wear it."

Without thinking, I pulled back my hand and licked the sauce from my finger. Willa's gaze followed, cheeks turning bright red as her eyes focused on my mouth.

I swallowed and shifted my body back, dropping my hand to my lap. What had I done? That had been entirely inappropriate. I glanced around the table but was thankful to find out that no one had been paying attention to us. Rose was too busy devouring fries and sighing with every bite while John gazed at her. The marquis was still staring down the burger even though he had taken a few nibbles.

I shot Willa a quick embarrassed smile.

She shook her head and squeezed my hand before returning to the food. "Don't worry, no one saw." She turned her gaze from me. "And I liked it."

Just as I took another bite of my burger, the doors to the dining room swung open, and in walked the butler.

"Sir, Ms. Melinda is here to see you." The marquis' butler stepped aside to reveal Melinda's curvy figure and head of bouncy curls.

The marquis, who usually remained rather reserved, always the picture of sophistication, lit up at the sight of her. The sight of Melinda and the marquis amused me; whenever they were together, the room filled with playful banter and subtle flirtation.

Melinda approached the dining table, and the marquis

greeted her warmly. However, he was not able to hide his curiosity. "Why did you not arrive with Willa and Anne?"

The marquis' question hung in the air, but before anyone could respond, Melinda spoke up. "Apologies for my tardiness." There was a mischievous glint in Melinda's eyes. "I had to take care of something before I could join you all."

I knew Melinda had planned to find something for the marquis while Willa and I were on our date; I wondered what it was.

The marquis pointed to the butler. "Can you pull out a chair beside me for Ms. Melinda?"

"My pleasure, sir." The butler moved to the table in swift struts, readying a chair for Melinda.

"Thank you," Melinda told the butler as she sat. The butler pushed her seat in and returned to his previous spot beside the entrance.

"You may go," the marquis said to the butler before returning his attention to Melinda. "Are you not hungry? We have all already started eating, but there is still plenty left."

"I'll take some fries."

The marquis reached forward, grabbed one of the cardboard boxes with potatoes, and handed it to Melinda.

Willa appeared joyful beside me. She was observing her father and Melinda with a keen eye, her face soft and wistful. Seeing Willa content and excited for her father's happiness settled my heart. Losing her mother had been a devastating blow for both her and her father. She'd confided in me about how much her father had still been grieving years after her mother's death. To witness her father opening up to another woman was undoubtedly a blessing.

Melinda set down the fries. "But first, I wanted to give you the reason I was late." She pulled a beautifully wrapped package from her skirt pocket. Neatly folded red paper covered the rectangular shape, held together with a bright white bow.

The marquis' eyes sparkled with anticipation as he accepted the gift. Ever so careful, he unwrapped it.

My curiosity was piqued, and I leaned forward. What had Melinda gifted the marquis?

From beneath the marquis' hands, a square, blue bottle emerged.

"Cologne," Melinda said in a soft tone.

"And something else, I see," the marquis answered in a burr. There was another item wrapped around the bottle of cologne. He slid the band up and over the glass. "Fascinating... a watch but unlike any I've seen before."

The marquis examined the burnished leather bands and the gleaming watch face with delight.

Melinda reached out and pointed towards it. "Turn it over and have a look."

The marquis obeyed, his eyes widening as he read the engraved message inside the timepiece out loud.

To my Marquis. Love, Melinda.

My heart skipped a beat as I witnessed this intimate gesture. How romantic. The significance of those words resonated through the room, and a warm glow of affection enveloped my heart. The marquis and Melinda were lost in their private moment, no thoughts spared for the rest of us sitting around the dining room table.

Willa whispered in my ear, "Melinda makes my father happy. How fortunate is he to have found someone again, and how fortunate are we to witness their blossoming connection?"

I had never considered myself a romantic, but seeing Melinda and Willa's father together stirred my heart and made me wonder what might be possible for me. At the very least, I hoped with her father in love that Willa would not feel as burdened. There were so many things I wanted to explore with her; I already looked forward to our next adventure with the Magical Bookshop.

20

Gentle And Soft

The air inside the Magical Bookshop hummed with anticipation as I joined Willa and Melinda amid ancient and newer tomes. The cozy space expanded, accommodating an impressive collection of books from all eras.

Willa stretched her arms. "What now? Are we traveling to another place again?"

Melinda crouched behind the counter, her curls disappearing beneath the dark wood. With a sneeze, she popped back up, a dusty book clutched in her hand. "Not today." She breathed in deeply, cheeks popping out, and exhaled firmly to blow the dust off the book. With most of the dust gone, she gave the binding a last good pat. "There, that looks better." She ambled toward a shelf in the back.

"Then what are we doing today?" Willa was still waiting for an answer and was getting a bit antsy.

"Today, the client is coming to us." Melinda added the

book to the shelf and turned back toward us. "I will make my-self scarce and let you handle whoever is stopping by today."

I frowned. "What—"

Melinda waved her hand. "Don't worry. There's nothing to it."

Willa crooked her brow, and Melinda let out a deep laugh. "Really. All you two need to do is mind the store, and when someone enters, help them with whatever they ask. The store will do the rest."

"All right..." I supposed we would have to learn on our own eventually.

Melinda moved to a bag hanging from a nail on the door to the small living quarter where she slept. "These are for you, something to wear that isn't so conspicuous." She pulled two dresses from the bag.

"You don't like our outfits?" Willa jested as she accepted one of the dresses.

"They look great. However, most of our visitors do not expect to see people wearing them, and we are in the business of serving them."

Willa and I quickly changed into the new dresses. They were thin and flowy, providing ample room to move about. I liked the way the fabric brushed my calves and cinched at my natural waist. It was different from the long empire gown I had been wearing, which pulled in right beneath my bosom. That style made me look even more rectangular than I already was.

I brushed my newly defined waist and felt a flutter of excitement at seeing a hint of a curve. Willa and I were oppo-sites; where she was all softness and curves, I was flat and angular. I admired Willa's feminine beauty. Everything about her drew me in and made me want to reach out and hold her.

I stopped and turned back to look at Melinda.

The atmosphere shifted. Melinda's necklace, a delicate pendant glimmering with an otherworldly radiance, began to pulsate against her chest. Then my necklace started pulsating as well. The pulsations sent ripples of anticipation through the air, signaling the imminent journey of the bookshop to a time and place where a fateful encounter would take place.

My heart skipped a beat, and my senses heightened. We were traveling to a new place and would soon be visited by a customer who had no idea they would be sent across time. I exchanged a knowing glance with Willa; her eyes reflected the shared understanding of the profound magic unfolding before our eyes. We had not yet become familiar with the rhythms and signs of this remarkable bookshop. All we knew was that it connected potential soulmates across time and space.

Thus far, the bookstore had seemed a fixed place, but now as the pulsations intensified, the shop transformed around us. The shelves blurred, shifting and rearranging themselves to suit what I assumed would be the desires of the approaching visitor. The familiar warmth of the bookstore dissipated, replaced by an otherworldly coolness.

"And that is my cue to leave." Melinda nodded and, touching her pendant, disappeared, leaving us alone.

My heart raced, the hairs on the back of my neck rising. I checked the rearranged shelves filled with different novels from the ones I had been thumbing through earlier. There were normal novels with titles on their spines, but now I also noticed multiple blank books. My fingertips brushed against a blue-covered one, a whisper of destiny tingling against my skin. I felt the urge to tip out the book and turn to a particular page or explore a specific passage, but I stopped myself before I did.

Amid my search, the bookshop settled into its new time and place. The air crackled with a different energy, vibrant and pulsating with a unique rhythm.

A small bell rang, and Willa and I glanced at each other. The visitor was here, and we would need to be ready to assist.

The door creaked open, revealing a figure clad in tight black pants and a short-sleeved shirt. The visitor's eyes widened with awe as they stepped inside, their gaze immediately drawn to Willa and me, the only constants in this strange bookshop.

Feeling the weight of the moment, I smiled warmly and extended a hand of welcome. "Welcome to our extraordinary bookshop. We've been expecting you." I hoped my voice conveyed comfort and assurance.

Beside me, Willa took a deep breath, steadying herself. With confident steps, she approached the visitor. "Welcome, my name is Willa, and I'm here to assist you."

The traveler's eyes widened, and she sucked in a breath. She moved closer with a small, disbelieving shake of her head. Her gaze darted around the shop, blinking at every turn.

"I... I'm not sure how I ended up here. I did not even know there was a bookstore here. You must be new."

Willa nodded empathetically, offering a reassuring smile. "Don't worry; you are exactly where you are meant to be. This bookshop has a way of guiding souls to their destined paths. It seems fate has brought you here for a reason."

"I can help you find what you are looking for," I told the visitor.

She bobbed her head and tightened the band holding her hair in a ponytail.

But Melinda had been right; there was not much for us to do. Within moments, the visitor began browsing the shelves, entranced by the secrets whispered by the pages, a magical pull urging her to explore their debts.

Willa watched, her grin growing wider by the second. Her excitement matched mine. This would be the first time I got to see what happened to one of the visitors—what happened to Rose.

The woman meandered through the collection, drawn to books that appeared to resonate with them, then moved on again.

And then, amidst the array of books, the visitor's eyes landed on a seemingly unremarkable volume—a small dusty blank book. She hesitated for a moment before reaching out to touch its smooth cover.

I sensed the significance of this moment, the pivotal choice that lay before the strange woman. She had more than likely woken up that morning thinking it was to be another unremarkable day, and now she was at the start of an adventure, one that might never let her come back to her own time again.

In less time than it took me to take a breath, the visitor opened the pages, and the world around them seemed to dissolve. I blinked at the sight, and then she was gone, leaving behind only the book now splayed open on the ground.

"Should we pick it up?" Willa hesitated, perhaps worried

she'd disappear into an unfamiliar time as well if she touched the pages.

"I think so. I believe the book is only meant for the soul mate; it is fair to assume that we are safe."

Willa pursed her lips. "I wonder where she's gone." Her green eyes met mine. "Do you think it will be someplace nice?"

Willa jumped as Melinda's voice sounded behind us. "Nothing is guaranteed."

I turned toward Melinda.

"The visitor could have gone anywhere, anytime, and while she is there, life continues as usual."

I frowned. That sounded dangerous. "What if they get into an accident? What happens to them, then? How do you know when to show up at their side?"

Melinda smiled and walked past me, squatting down to pick up the abandoned book. "Let's take a look, shall we?"

Confused, I glanced at Willa. We both sidled in on opposite sides of Melinda, who turned the book to the first page. My eyes widened as dots of ink appeared on the blank pages. The color saturated until the blurry spots turned into sentences I could read.

"Watch closely." Melinda pointed at the first paragraph, eyes sparkling.

I leaned in closer to the book while more and more words appeared until the entire page was filled.

"It's winter, and she slipped on some ice." Willa gasped. "This book will hold her entire story?"

It was mesmerizing to watch the visitor's story materialize before my very eyes, paragraph by paragraph. I wondered how many pages would be written before she met her potential soul mate.

As if hearing my thoughts, Melinda continued, "The book guides her to the time and place, but the timing and circumstances will be left to the whims of fate. Sometimes it takes only a few days, while for others, it may be weeks before their destinies align."

"Weeks?"

"Yes, but I have their book. That is how I will know when to show up. Everything she experiences will be documented here."

"And what happens when she meets her potential soul mate?" Willa asked, her voice tinged with curiosity.

Melinda's gaze held profound wisdom. "When the time is right, I will visit the woman and present her with a choice. She can choose to stay in that time with her newfound love or return to her own era. It will be a decision she must make based on her heart's desires."

Melinda closed the pages and patted the top of the binding. "In the end, if she chooses to return to her own time, she will get to keep this."

My brain whirred. That's right; they can choose to return and leave their soulmates behind. "How often does that happen?"

Melinda returned the book to the nearest shelf. "Not often, most choose to stay with whomever they've fallen in love with, but it does happen."

Willa shook her head, brows furrowed. "Who would ever leave the person they love?"

Her vehement tone of voice sent a pang through my heart.

Willa was an only child and never had to consider her family, but I had Mary and Randolph to think about. Adding on to that, I had my mother to consider as well; she had not been the same since my father passed. My family meant the world to me, and I could not let them down, even if it meant turning away from my wants and needs.

Did she think I was a coward for not admitting my feelings as honestly and openly as she did? Every wonderful stolen moment with Willa already wracked me with guilt because I had stopped looking for a suitor to help my family. Willa entranced my mind; whenever she was near, I had no thoughts of anything else. I wanted to spend every waking moment with her. See her laugh and cry. Our time at the Magical Bookshop felt like a dream, our universe where nothing existed but us. I only hoped the dream would not end.

Melinda shrugged. "There are many reasons, most of them very personal. I can only guide them, but it is their individual choices that can change their lives in a myriad of ways."

Chewing my lip, I considered Melinda's words. "Rose's grandmother returned. Do you know why?"

"I'm afraid that was before my time."

Willa uncrossed her arms, and her gaze slipped to me. "I would have never left." She pressed in closer to my side, her fingers reaching for mine and curling around them. She squeezed my hand, her expression shimmering with tenderness. Without a single spoken syllable, I understood the depth of her meaning. My heart leaped in my throat.

Perhaps this was it. Perhaps the Magical Bookshop had given me my soul mate as well. Was it too much to hope that

I could forget about my family's prospects? Was it too much to ask that Randolph take responsibility?

My heart felt settled—even-keeled—when I looked at Willa. I wondered about the challenges and hoped for the potential of our love story yet to unfold.

Willa nudged me out of my musings. "Let us straighten the shelves."

Together, we delved further into the depths of the book-shop, fingers entwined as we brushed past the newly arranged shelves. Briefly, I wondered if, in the quiet corners of a different shop, another blank book waited, ready to inscribe our tale.

Though every thought fled my mind when Willa turned and brushed her lips against mine. Hidden between the books, she kissed me. First gentle and soft, then harder. Her sweet breath mingled with mine felt like a promise, sealing the words she had said before. And I? I wanted it all. I just needed assurance that I could.

21

Updates From Home

Leaning back against the pillows on my bed, I brushed my fingertips along my lips. My heart fluttered whenever I thought of Willa's lips against mine. I should have readied myself for the day an hour ago, but I had been too preoccupied with replaying the happenings of the previous day. My mind had been buzzing with thoughts until late in the evening.

I yawned and swung back the thick blanket covering me. Picking at the strand holding my braided hair together, I ambled to the stool in front of my vanity. With quick movements, I undid my snarled hair and brushed it back into a state of compliance.

I had not heard Estelle, the French maid, pass by the corridor. Perhaps she was busy elsewhere; helping in the kitchen, serving Rose and John in the dining room, or fetching something from the shops. It did not matter. I was perfectly capable of dressing myself.

Shrugging off my nightgown, I grabbed a small cloth towel and dipped it into the water bowl on top of the vanity. Using the edge of the cloth, I dabbed at my sleep-covered eyelids, then freshened my entire face.

Much better.

I glanced at my face in the mirror; my eyes still appeared a bit tired, but the cool water helped liven up my cheeks. All that was left was to refasten my hair.

A mere half hour later, I made my way downstairs.

I entered the elegant dining room, the soft morning light filtering through the lace curtains and casting a warm glow on the polished mahogany table. Rose and John were still seated, their postures relaxed as they enjoyed each other's company. Rose, with her delicate frame adorned in a flowing muslin gown, looked radiant despite the early hour. John, ever the gentleman, sat beside her, adding sugar to her tea.

"Good morning, Anne!" Rose waved to me with a cheerful smile, her other hand resting tenderly upon her growing belly. "Please, join us."

"Good morning, Rose. Good morning, John." I settled into my chair; the aroma of freshly baked bread and fragrant tea filled the air, tantalizing my senses. A maid, dressed in a crisp apron and cap, approached with a silver teapot, her footsteps silent upon the parquet floor.

"Shall I pour you some tea, Miss Anne?" The maid lifted the arm holding the teapot.

"Yes, please." I extended my porcelain teacup toward her. She poured the fragrant liquid, its steam swirling upwards, casting a gentle mist over the delicate china.

Rose swallowed a bit of bread and tipped her head

towards me. "Thank you again for inviting us over to Bambreich Manor and bringing fast food. I hadn't even realized how much I'd missed the taste of home. Not that I ate burgers all the time, but I sure miss being able to go through a drive-through on the way home and bite into a greasy burger."

John smiled at Rose and patted her upper back in soft, gentle strokes. "I wish I could have experienced your time as well."

"I am glad you enjoyed it. Perhaps Willa and I will be able to bring back other things now and again. You could always let me know if there is anything specific you would like."

Rose's eyes crinkled, and she looked a bit bashful. "That leads me to another question. Will you and Willa travel to the future again any time soon? I...Well, I would like my family to know about..." Rose's gaze turned tender as she placed a hand on her rounded belly. "We are blessed, and before the end of the year, we shall welcome a new member into our family. The only thing missing is the knowledge that my mother and father know they have a grandchild on the way."

John nodded. "And I am missing my best friend; had he been here, I would have named him the godfather."

I could understand their sentiments. If I had been pregnant, I would have wanted everyone I love to know as well. "I can speak with Melinda and Willa. Perhaps I can convey a message to Austin and William when we travel there."

"Thank you." Rose's face lit up.

I sipped my tea, savoring its warmth and the comforting camaraderie of our conversation. It had been awkward at first, but I was glad for the ease with which we interacted with one another now.

Just as I reached for a piece of buttered toast, a distinct knock resonated through the hallway, interrupting the tranquility of the room. I glanced up, curiosity piqued by the unexpected sound. A moment later, the dining room door creaked open, revealing the presence of the young maid.

"Pardon the intrusion, Miss Anne," she began, her voice a bit breathless. "But your brother has arrived. He awaits you in the foyer."

My heart skipped a beat at the mention of my brother's arrival. With a swift motion, I pushed back my chair, a surge of anticipation flooding my veins. "Thank you," I managed to say, my voice tinged with excitement. I had not seen Randolph in a while and was hoping for news about my mother and sister.

I hurried my way to the foyer, the elegant surroundings fading into a blur as my anticipation grew. The clicking of my shoes on the marble floor echoed through the hallway, matching the rapid rhythm of my heart.

As I rounded the corner, there he stood, my dear brother, Randolph, tall and dashing in his tailored coat and cravat. His eyes brightened as he caught sight of me, a warm smile spreading across his face. We hugged, the familiar scent of his cologne enveloping me in a comforting embrace.

"Anne, my dear sister," he murmured, his voice filled with affection. "How I've missed you."

"Randolph, it's been far too long."

He gently pulled away, his hands resting on my shoulders as he studied my face. "You look well, Anne. London society certainly suits you."

A smile tugged at the corners of my lips as I glanced

down at my modest gown, the delicate fabric and understated elegance befitting the times. "Thank you, dear brother. I have missed you terribly. Pray, tell me, what brings you to our doorstep?"

Randolph's eyes gleamed with mischief, his voice brimming with excitement. "I have news, Anne. News that shall brighten your day. But first, invite your brother into the warmth of the dining room. I'm famished."

I chuckled, then called out for the maid. "Would you kindly bring some more tea and refreshments to the dining room?" After leading Randolph to the dining room, I pointed him toward a pair of comfortable chairs opposite Rose and John.

"Welcome, Randolph," John said.

"Thank you for having me." Randolph swept aside the tails of his coat and settled down on the plush seat.

I could not wait anymore. "Tell me, Randolph, how is Mother? And what news from Westbridge? Is Mary doing well?"

Randolph's face softened, a fondness shining in his eyes. "Mother is in good health, my dear sister. She sends her love, and Mary is thriving. She has taken on a new hobby of painting and has shown quite the talent."

My heart swelled with pride for my sister and gratitude for the updates from home. It had been some time since I had seen my mother and sister, and their presence in my thoughts warmed my heart.

The sound of approaching footsteps heralded the maid's arrival, carrying a tray adorned with a steaming teapot and an assortment of delectable treats to supplement the bread already present. She placed it on the table before us, her presence as graceful as ever.

"Thank you," I said with a grateful smile. The maid retreated, and I poured tea for Randolph and myself, relishing the familiar ritual that brought comfort and a sense of home.

As we indulged in sips of tea, the conversation took a turn toward Beth and how she recently eloped to Ireland with a man who had claimed to be a duke. Randolph's brows furrowed with concern as he inquired about her well-being.

"Tell me, Anne, have you received any news regarding Beth? Is she safe? Is she happy?" His voice was laced with worry.

"Indeed, Randolph, we have received a letter from Beth. She managed to escape the authorities and safely arrived in Ireland. Though her circumstances may have been unconventional, she sounds positively elated."

A smile tugged at Randolph's lips as the weight of worry lifted from his shoulders. "I'm glad to hear that she's safe and content. Please convey my regards and well wishes to her when you have the chance."

I nodded, making a mental note to pass along Randolph's message to Beth. It was a relief to know that my dear friend had found solace and happiness, even if the path she had taken had been fraught with uncertainties.

Leaning back in my chair, I braced herself for the inevitable question that had become a constant refrain from Randolph's lips. But to my surprise, when he spoke, his tone carried a different cadence, lacking the usual insistence.

"And what about you, Anne? Have you found a suitor yet?" His voice sounded softer, filled with a touch of resignation.

I met his gaze, determination no doubt evident in my eyes. "No, Randolph, I haven't found a suitor yet."

A flicker of understanding passed through Randolph's eyes, his rigid back softening. "Perhaps I have been too insistent, Anne. I only wish for your well-being and the prosperity of our family. If you have found contentment in your own way, I will trust in your judgment."

I had been ready to defend myself, thinking of arguments about why I had not managed a match yet, puffing myself up so much that his words nearly deflated me.

"My judgment?"

Randolph smiled and nodded. "Yes, your judgment. I will defer to the decisions you make about your own life. There's no need to follow through with the reason for your stay in London."

No reason? Why would there no longer be a reason to find a suitor? "Why? What is the good news you mentioned?"

Randolph grinned, dimples forming on his cheeks. "I have been hired to be a solicitor at a small law firm in Westbridge. Now, I will need to be trained first, so money remains tight. However, I imagine I shall soon be able to make large payments towards the debt. It is not the fastest way, but now you won't need to marry some sad fop in haste to save our hides."

I was speechless. "A job?"

"Yes."

"I won't need to marry?"

"Not unless you want to." Randolph wiggled his eyebrows at me, teasing me.

A surge of emotions swelled within my chest, a blend of relief, gratitude, and a touch of disbelief. I looked into my brother's eyes, searching for any sign of uncertainty or hesitation.

"Really? You mean it?" My heart surged with a mixture of hope and cautious optimism.

Randolph nodded, a soft smile tugging at his lips. "Yes, Anne. I mean it. This opportunity holds promise, and I am committed to fulfilling our family's obligations. I appreciate your dedication and sacrifice, and I have come to realize that it is time for you to make choices about your wants and desires in life."

Tears welled up in my eyes, threatening to spill over. The weight that had burdened my shoulders for so long began to lift, replaced by a newfound sense of freedom and possibility. And all I could see was Willa. I could be there forever with Willa.

I threw my arms around Randolph, embracing him tightly. "Thank you, Randolph. Thank you for understanding and for giving me a chance to choose my path. I am grateful for your support and your commitment to our family."

Randolph returned the embrace, his own emotions evident in the strength of his hold. "Be careful, Anne, and choose wisely. But above all, I want you to be happy. It is time for you to forge your destiny."

I pulled back slightly, my eyes meeting Randolph's. "I will, Randolph. I will make choices with both caution and conviction. And I will cherish the freedom and opportunity that you have granted me."

22

All The Time In The World

The sun was high in the sky, casting a warm glow over the bustling streets of the unfamiliar city. Willa and I strolled arm in arm, marveling at the sights and sounds of this modern world we found ourselves in. It was a stark contrast to the Regency era we had left behind.

At least London in the future still had been recognizable; most buildings echoed back to our own time, albeit with a different spin. This American city, however, seemed alien; all tall, sleek structures with tons of windows and bright flashing lights on screens.

"Anne, do you think we shall ever get used to this place?" Willa's eyes grew bright with wonder.

I smiled, feeling a mix of excitement and trepidation. "I

cannot say for certain, Willa. But the possibilities are endless, are they not?"

As we walked along the crowded street, I felt a lightness in my heart. There was something I needed to confide in Willa; I had not yet said anything about my brother's visit.

Taking a deep breath, I turned to face her. "Willa, I must tell you something." I could not keep a smile from forming on my face. "Yesterday, my brother Randolph visited me. He informed me that he has secured a position as a solicitor for a small law firm in Westbridge."

Willa's eyes widened, and she squeezed my arm in excitement. "Oh, Anne! That is splendid news! Does it mean that your family will no longer be burdened by debts?"

I nodded, a mix of relief and uncertainty flooding over me. "Indeed, Willa. With Randolph's newfound employment, our family will be free of financial worries. Our debts shall be paid in due time."

My smile grew wider. I knew what this meant for me. I had always been the dutiful daughter, ready to marry for the sake of our family's fortune. But now, with the burden lifted, I did not need to seek out a suitor.

"Willa, it means that I do not need to marry for financial security. Randolph's earnings will take care of everything. I shall be free to follow my own path."

Willa's face softened, her eyes searching mine. "And what path is that, Anne?"

I took a deep breath, the words escaping my lips before I could stop them. "It is a path that leads to you, Willa. I have promised your father that I would watch out for you, and I aim to do just that." I raised my arms to the sky, waving them around us. "I want this to be our life."

Willa's eyes widened, but a gentle smile graced her lips. Her lashes fluttered as she averted her gaze. "Anne, you cannot imagine how happy that makes me. I have to admit, I wondered if you were as serious about me as I am about you. I... Thank you." She placed her palm on the side of my face and leaned in to place a quick peck on my lips. Then, blushing, she retreated.

Relief washed over me. My heart surged and fluttered. The weight that burdened me had lifted, and in its place, there was hope and the promise of a future with the woman I loved.

But there was one more matter I needed to discuss, one that concerned John and Rose. "Willa, before I found out about Randolph's employment, Rose asked me to deliver some news to William. She wants him and her family to know that she and John are expecting a child."

Willa's eyes sparkled with delight. "Oh, how wonderful! Is that why we are in this city? Does William live here?" She chuckled. "I had wondered why you were so insistent on traveling to America."

"I wanted to keep it a bit of a surprise." I lifted my brow and winked. "But we shall visit William a bit later; I had something else in mind first." I patted my pocket, which held a sleek piece of plastic. "Another surprise, courtesy of Melinda. She said that the magic of the shop provides the financial means necessary to us."

Grabbing Willa's hand, I headed for our first destination.

Stepping into the grand department store, I couldn't help but feel a mix of awe and excitement. The polished marble floors stretched out before us, and the towering shelves filled with countless treasures beckoned. Willa's eyes sparkled with anticipation as we entered this modern emporium of fashion.

"Willa, can you believe the sheer magnitude of this place?" My voice was filled with amazement. "It is as if we have stepped into a world of its own."

Willa's smile was infectious, her red curls bouncing with each step. "Indeed, Anne. It's like a treasure trove of garments waiting to be discovered. Shall we explore together?"

With a nod, I followed Willa's lead, weaving through the aisles of clothing racks. The vibrant colors and exquisite fabrics dazzled my senses. The sheer variety of clothing options was overwhelming, and I couldn't help but feel a surge of excitement course through me.

The shop attendant, a friendly young woman with a warm smile, approached us. "Hello there. Can I assist you in finding anything specific?"

Willa grinned mischievously and turned to me. "Oh, Anne, let's ask her for some recommendations. We can indulge in a little fashion adventure!"

I chuckled, finding the idea quite thrilling. "Very well, let's see what she suggests."

The shop attendant, whose nametag read 'Emma,' took note of our distinct appearances. I, with my slender frame, porcelain skin, angular features, and dark brown hair framing my face, while Willa stood by my side, her voluptuous and curvy figure accentuated by her fiery red hair, green eyes, and a sprinkle of freckles across her cheeks.

"Ah, I have just the thing for you two!" There was a glint of excitement in Emma's eyes. She scurried off and returned with a selection of garments, a mix of classic and contemporary styles.

"This is for you." Emma held up an ivory blouse that caught my eye. "I think this will complement your skin tone beautifully, and it's perfect for casual and more formal occasions."

I took the blouse into my hands, feeling the softness of the fabric. It was exquisite. "Thank you. It's lovely."

Willa's eyes sparkled as Emma turned to her. "And for you, I have a vibrant emerald-green dress that will accentuate your curves wonderfully. The color will make your red hair shine even brighter."

Willa held the dress against her form, admiring the way it draped. "Oh, it's stunning! I cannot wait to try it on."

As we continued to browse, Emma guided us through the different sections, suggesting pieces that reflected our styles. The two of us laughed and chatted as we experimented with different looks. The joy in Willa's eyes mirrored my own as we immersed ourselves in this delightful fashion escapade.

"I think we are ready to try these on," Willa said to me, flashing me a smile, her hands overflowing with clothing. She turned to the shop attendant. "Are there any dressing rooms?"

Emma pointed. "To the left of the clothing section, around the purse counter."

"Thank you," Willa answered, and together we looked for a place to try on our new blouses, dresses, and shoes.

Right where the shop attendant had pointed us, we found a row of changing rooms, black drapes blocking the inside from sight. I turned to enter one, but Willa grasped my wrist.

"I would like you to change with me." Willa pulled me into one of the open spaces and closed the black drapes behind us.

With a trembling hand, I began to undress, peeling away the layers of the dress I borrowed from Melinda. My heart fluttered with nervous anticipation, my thoughts swirling with a mixture of desire and uncertainty. I had always been a modest and proper lady, accustomed to changing in the presence of maids. But this was different. This was Willa, the woman who had captured my heart and ignited a flame within me like no other.

As I stood in my undergarments, my cheeks grew hot. The thought of Willa undressing me, touching me, awakened a torrent of emotions within me. I hesitated, my hands frozen, unsure of how to proceed.

It was then that I felt the soft brush of Willa's fingertips against my arm, and my breath caught in my throat. Willa's voice, filled with tenderness, broke through the hazy whirlwind of my thoughts.

"Anne, may I... may I help you with your stays?" Willa asked, her voice gentle and laden with unspoken desire.

My eyes met Willa's in the mirror, our gazes locked, a magnetic pull drawing us closer. At that moment, all doubts and inhibitions melted away, replaced by a raw, unyielding longing.

Unable to find my voice, I nodded, lips parting in silent agreement. As Willa's hands deftly worked to loosen the laces of my stays, my skin tingled with each touch, my body responding to the proximity of the woman I loved.

The room disappeared around me, the outside world fading into insignificance as the connection between us deepened. Desire and vulnerability intermingled within my being, an intoxicating cocktail of sensations that left me breathless.

As the corset finally fell away, I turned to face Willa, her eyes filled with a mixture of adoration and longing. With a soft, barely audible gasp, I leaned forward, my lips brushing against Willa's in a delicate, tender kiss.

Willa's fingers reached around my bare back, sliding up and down, sending shivers down my skin.

"Let me help you try something on," I told Willa. "Sit down on the bench."

Willa followed my command. I grabbed a pair of knee-high boots made from supple, light brown leather. Kneeling between her legs, I slid off the pair of velvet slippers she had been wearing, small marks of wear and tear on the bottom. I grabbed one of her elegantly arched feet and slid it into the boot. Ever so slowly, I pulled the zipper up, tightening the leather around her creamy calves until I reached her knee. She was still wearing her dress, its hem brushing my knuckles. I paused, tipping my head up to gaze at Willa's face.

Willa chewed her lower lip, redness blooming all across her freckled face as she gazed back at me. I loved to see her flustered. Dipping my hand below the hem of her dress, I trailed my fingers up the inside of her thighs.

"Did everything fit all right?" a feminine voice spoke from outside the dressing room—Emma, the shop attendant.

Cursed timing.

Willa pulled me back to standing, arms weaving around me.

"Yes, we are still trying on a few things, thank you." Willa's voice rang out in an embarrassed squeak.

I giggled, and Willa covered my mouth with her hand

in one swoop, embarrassment coloring her cheeks an even deeper red than before.

I was grateful that the shop attendant acquiesced, and we heard her footsteps trail away.

With a soft squeeze on Willa's upper arm, I looked into her eyes. "It's all right. We have all the time in the world." Willa's worried expression softened, and she nodded, her eyes conveying a mix of relief and desire.

Leaning in, I captured Willa's lips in a last tender kiss before we tried on the clothing we had gathered. There would be time for more exploration. For now, my promise to Rose and John was waiting.

23

William And Austin

My stomach fluttered when the door swung open and revealed William's familiar face. I bounced on my feet, exchanging a glance with Willa, both of us aware of the surprise we were about to spring upon my friend.

"William." A smile spread across my face. "It's been far too long since we last met."

His eyes widened in astonishment, his mouth agape. "Anne? What in the world... How did you get here? I had no idea you were involved with the Magical Bookshop and time traveling." His gaze turned to Willa. "And who is this? I don't believe we've had the pleasure of meeting before, but you do look quite familiar."

Willa's eyes twinkled as she shook his hand. "Likewise, William. Perhaps we crossed paths at a ball once. It's a pleasure to meet you. I've heard a lot about you."

William smirked and crooked his brow. "All good things, I hope."

Willa grinned. "Of course, I would not have mentioned it otherwise."

I chuckled; William had always been a charmer. "Oh, William, there is so much we have to tell you. But first, may we come in?"

William snapped out of his initial surprise, his face lighting up with delight. "Of course. Please, come in." He waved at us to follow him. "You must have quite the tale to share."

We stepped inside the cozy apartment, enjoying the decorated space. I could tell where William had left his mark with poetry books left on furniture and art on the walls. The scent of baked goods permeated the place. Austin's voice reached our ears before he joined us in the living room, a smile mirroring William's.

"Well, well, what a delightful surprise." Austin extended his hand to shake ours. "I don't think I've had the pleasure."

"Willa Balfour," Willa said as she shook his hand.

"Nice to meet you. It is a surprise to see anyone that William knows...from his own time."

William offered us seats and then disappeared into the kitchen. He returned moments later, bearing a tray holding drinks and the baked goods I had smelled. Apple tarts, if I guessed right.

"Please, help yourselves," he said with a warm smile. "So, tell us, how have you both been? And what brings you here from the Regency era?"

I took a sip of my soda, the cool bubbles tickling my throat in a most delightful way. "We've been well, William, thank you. Willa and I exchanged a glance before I continued. "Melinda has been planning on passing on the responsibilities of the Magical Bookshop, and she chose us as her successors."

William's surprise was evident in his widened eyes and dropped jaw. "You mean to say... you're taking over the Magical Bookshop? That is extraordinary."

I nodded. With a smile, I took a sip of soda and set my glass down on the coffee table, my fingers tracing the rim. William's eyes sparkled as he leaned forward, his attention focused on Willa and me.

"As for the reason for our visit, it is connected to Rose and John. You see, Rose asked me to stop by..."

Austin leaned forward, his eyes gleaming with curiosity. "Rose? What did she want?"

Willa's face lit up as she met William and Austin's gaze. "Rose and John have entrusted us with a special message for you. They wanted us to tell you that they are expecting a child."

William's eyes widened, a bright smile appearing on his face. "A child? Oh, how wonderful." He shook his head and laughed. "Please convey my heartfelt congratulations to them."

I nodded, smiling as well. "Indeed, it is a joyous occasion. And that's not all, William. Rose specifically mentioned that she would be honored if you would consider being the child's godfather."

The smile on William's face vanished, replaced by a look of shock; I could see the emotions welling up within him. "Me? A godfather? It would be my utmost honor. Please assure Rose and John that I will fulfill this role with all my heart."

Willa reached out and touched William's hand. "They knew that you would be the perfect choice, William."

A smile played on William's lips as he nodded. "Thank you, both of you. This means more to me than words can express." Austin smiled and wrapped his arm around William.

Taking a moment to savor the sweetness of the apple tart, I turned my attention back to William. "There is one more thing. Rose expressed her wish for her mother and father to hear the news of her pregnancy. She hopes that they can share in the excitement."

An understanding look crossed William's face as he contemplated Rose's desire. "I understand her longing. It has been a while since she and her parents have spoken. I will do everything in my power to make sure they receive this wonderful news."

Willa's gaze softened, her voice filled with compassion. "Your support in this matter means the world to Rose, William. I know she treasures your friendship."

William smiled broadly at Willa, then after swallowing a sip of soda, he leaned forward toward me. His eyes sparkled with curiosity.

"Anne, I haven't heard any news about Beth in quite some time. How has she been faring?"

A small smile played on my lips as I prepared to share the surprising turn of events that had unfolded in Beth's life. "Oh, William, you won't believe it. Beth has embarked on quite the adventure. She eloped to Ireland with a man who had been pretending to be an Irish duke."

William's eyebrows shot up in astonishment, a mixture of amusement and concern crossing his features. "Goodness,

Anne. Is she all right? Did she know he was pretending all along? I can only imagine what John has been feeling."

I reassured him with a nod, my heart lighter as I shared the story. "Beth is safe. She discovered his deception not long after. Willa and I have very much been kept in the loop. If it had not been for Willa, Beth would never have met Henry—the fake duke. Thankfully, Beth managed to evade the constables who were pursuing them on their way to Ireland. And, well, despite the initial deception, Beth is quite smitten with the man. She's found herself very much in love."

William burst into laughter, the sound filling the room. "That is so like Beth. Always finding herself in the most remarkable situations. I'm relieved to hear she's safe, though. Love has a way of leading us down unexpected paths." His eyes crinkled, and he flashed Austin a quick smile. "I would know."

I joined in William's laughter, the lightheartedness contagious. "Indeed, it does. Beth has always been an adventurer at heart, unafraid to chase her desires. I have no doubt she'll navigate her new relationship with equal determination. Ireland better watch out."

"That reminds me, and before I forget..." William stood from the couch, his movements purposeful, and made his way to a dresser adorned with vibrant plants. Opening one drawer, he carefully retrieved a small box.

Intrigued, I watched as he returned to his seat and handed the box to me with a smile. "Anne, this is a gift for Rose from her mother. It's something she gave me on the off chance that I'd see Rose again."

Taking the box into my hands, I felt my spirits rise. Rose

would be delighted to receive something from her family. The weight of the gesture and the connection it symbolized resonated within me. "Thank you, William. I will make sure this reaches Rose. I'm sure it will mean a great deal to her."

William's eyes softened, his gaze distant for a moment as he reminisced. "Rose's mother wanted her to know that she is loved, even if they are physically apart. It's a small token, but it will serve as a symbol of their connection. That despite the distance in time, they are still family."

"I will be sure to convey that message to Rose, William. I know it will bring her comfort."

A smile tugged at the corners of William's lips. "And please, tell Rose that her mother and father adored the portrait they received of her and John."

I nodded. "I will relay that message as well. I'm certain it will bring joy to Rose, knowing that her parents cherish their memories and hold her close to their hearts even if they are in different times."

***

My heart pounded with anticipation as Rose opened the small box. The room seemed to hold its breath as Rose's eyes widened with recognition, her hands trembling ever so slightly as she set aside a letter. I watched as Rose gasped.

"It's... it's my grandmother's wedding ring." Rose breathed deeply, her eyes welling up with tears. "I can't believe it."

John, his eyes filled with emotion, pulled Rose into a tight embrace, his arms encircling her protectively. The love between them radiated out.

Willa and I, both moved by the significance of the moment, offered our heartfelt words.

"It's beautiful, Rose," Willa said. "A precious heirloom to carry with you."

With trembling hands, Rose picked up and unfolded the letter, her voice shaking as she began to read the words written by her mother.

The letter spoke of her parents' love and their bittersweet farewell. It expressed their hope for Rose's happiness and their deep gratitude for the portrait sent by William and Austin.

I couldn't help but smile at the mention of the disbelief they had felt, the notion of their daughter living in a different era seeming like a fantastical tale.

But it was the last words of the letter that brought a collective hush to the room. Rose's voice trembled as she read aloud, her words filled with love and longing.

"Your grandmother would have wanted you to have her wedding ring." Rose's voice softened and filled with emotion. "To wear it when you find your true love."

Silence enveloped them, the weight of those words hanging in the air. Rose looked down at the ring in her hand, its golden band and ruby stone gleaming with timeless beauty. Slowly, she slid the ring onto her finger; it fit perfectly, as if it had always belonged there.

24

Anticipation

Leaving Rose and John to enjoy their private moment, Willa and I stepped out of the room and found ourselves in the elegant foyer. The hushed ambiance of the house surrounded us, echoing the love and happiness that still lingered in the air.

As we stood there, catching our breath and reflecting on the beautiful occasion, Willa turned to me with a mischievous glimmer in her eyes. "Anne, my father is away on a business trip, and Bambreich Manor is empty for the evening. I was wondering, would you like to share a carriage and spend the night at my home?"

A gentle smile tugged at the corners of my lips as the invitation danced in the air. The thought of spending the night in Willa's company, embraced by the tranquility of her family's estate, filled my heart with anticipation. Now that I had confessed that I was no longer in need of a marriage match, something had shifted and deepened between us. I wanted the chance to explore our changing relationship.

"Oh, Willa, yes." Perhaps I had sounded breathier than intended because Willa averted her gaze, a glimmer of a smile playing on her lips.

As we made our way towards the waiting carriage, the anticipation of the evening ahead enveloped us. The clatter of hooves against cobblestones resonated in the stillness of the night, guiding us toward our destination.

Inside the carriage, the soft glow of the lanterns cast a warm, golden hue, creating an intimate atmosphere as we settled into our seats. The gentle sway of the carriage matched the rhythm of our conversation as we shared laughter, dreams, and whispered secrets.

The journey to Bambreich Manor felt like a dance, the world outside fading into the background as we enjoyed the company of each other.

As the carriage came to a stop in front of the grand entrance to Bambreich Manor, a sense of enchantment filled the air. Together, we stepped out, our footsteps echoing in the quiet night. Willa led the way, her presence guiding me through the halls of her home until we arrived at the parlor.

The soft glow of candlelight bathed the space, casting dancing shadows on the walls. We settled onto a plush sofa, side by side, as anticipation hummed in the air.

A maid, clad in a neat uniform, entered the room with a warm smile. "Good evening, Miss Willa, Miss Anne. I've brought a candle to provide additional light."

Willa nodded in appreciation, her eyes sparkling. "Thank you, Martha. That would be lovely."

Martha lit the candle on a nearby table, casting a soft, warm glow that enhanced the intimate atmosphere. With a graceful curtsy, she took her leave, leaving us alone in the flickering light.

Willa turned towards me, her eyes brimming with excitement. "Anne, let's enjoy a light meal together, shall we? Martha, our maid, knows just what we need."

I nodded, my heart fluttering with anticipation. "That sounds wonderful, Willa. I'm looking forward to sharing this special moment with you."

Moments later, Martha returned, carrying a tray adorned with an assortment of grapes, cheese, and sliced bread. Two crystal glasses of wine completed the tableau, their ruby contents shimmering in the candlelight. With a gentle smile, Martha placed the tray on a nearby table and quietly exited the room, leaving us to our privacy.

As we settled in, our fingers brushed lightly against each other, a spark of electricity passing between us. Our eyes locked, and a shared smile filled the space between us. It was in that moment, as the room grew hushed and time appeared to stand still, that the air brimmed with sweet anticipation.

Taking a grape between my fingers, I offered it to Willa, my voice filled with a playful tone. "Care for a taste?"

Willa's lips curved into a mischievous smile as she leaned closer, her eyes gleaming with a mixture of desire and affection. "Oh, Anne, I believe I do."

Finishing up our bites of food and tipping back the last of the wine, Willa stood. Willa's eyes met mine, a glimmer of anticipation dancing within them. With a coy smile playing on her lips, she held out her hand, an unspoken invitation hanging in the air.

"Anne," she murmured, her voice soft and filled with affection, "are you ready to join me upstairs?"

My heart quickened its pace, matching the rhythm of my thoughts. At that moment, the weight of our connection, the tenderness that had blossomed between us, danced on the precipice of something more profound. With a flutter of nerves and a surge of love, I reached out and clasped her hand in mine.

"Yes, Willa," I whispered, my voice betraying a mix of shyness and excitement. "I'm ready."

Together, our hands entwined, we began our ascent up the grand staircase of Bambreich Manor. The steps beneath our feet felt solid and steady, echoing our journey toward an intimate space we both longed to explore.

As we reached the top of the stairs, Willa led me down a corridor adorned with exquisite paintings and lush tapestries, the luxury of her surroundings mirroring the blossoming emotions within our hearts. We walked in comfortable silence, our gazes occasionally meeting and veiling our expressions with a tender blend of shyness and desire.

Arriving at the door to Willa's room, the air hummed with anticipation. With a gentle push, she swung the door open, revealing her sanctuary. The room, bathed in soft, golden light, exuded an air of intimacy, inviting us to surrender to the depths of our affection.

The soft carpet beneath our feet offered a luxurious path toward the center of the room, where a plush, inviting bed awaited. We stood there, our eyes locked, our breaths mingling, the intensity of our connection palpable.

In that sacred moment, time slowed. The world outside faded into insignificance, leaving only the undeniable pull between Willa and me. I recognized that we were both shy, aware of the vulnerability that awaited us.

With an unspoken understanding, we closed the distance between us, our bodies magnetically drawn together. The air was charged with the sweet tension of anticipation as we indulged in the intoxicating dance of desire and affection. We reveled in the delicate balance between passion and tenderness, the unspoken promise of what lay ahead.

In Willa's bedroom, our love whispered through glances and gentle touches flourished in the gentle caress of Willa's hand and the steady beat of our hearts. This night, this union of souls would forever mark a turning point in our lives.

We took our time undressing, my heart surging every time I gazed at Willa. She was so incredibly beautiful, and she wanted *me*. She beckoned me towards her, patting the space beside her on the bed. I joined her atop the pretty coverlet, reaching out to graze her shoulders, arms, and breasts. Gently and lightly, exploring every part of her.

"Anne," she murmured, her breath hot against my ear, sliding her tongue along the rounded grooves and nipping down at the fleshy part on the bottom. Her hands found my skin as well, sliding down the nape of my neck and the curve of my spine until they landed at the swell of my bottom. My skin heated, tingling wherever her touch moved. "Will you touch me?"

My heart beat faster at her request, words freezing in

my mouth. I nodded softly, knowing she'd understand my agreement. I kissed her lips, then, taking her by surprise, I slid down, lowering myself to the bottom of the bed until my head lay against her navel. I exhaled softly, disturbing the faint shimmer of peach fuzz coating her belly. Everything about her entranced me.

She shivered beneath me, and I reached out, following the trail of goosebumps rising along her smooth skin. I had never imagined I would find myself tangled in bed with Willa, but I imagined there was no finer place to be.

Willa gasped when I slid my fingers further down, touching her at the apex of her thighs, her flesh like ripe fruit in my hand. I wanted to explore her curves and hear her repeat those sweet little gasps. She grasped my hair, keeping us connected as I moved to taste, my body heating at the prospect.

We spent what felt like hours taking turns touching each other, but finally, Willa collapsed into my arms, her skin slicked in sweat, a rosy sheen covering every part of her. She nudged my nose with her own and kissed me, burrowing herself deeper into my embrace.

"I love you." Her green eyes peered into mine, her face serene and glowing.

"I love you, too." I squeezed her tighter, burying my face in the crook of her neck, inhaling her sweet scent.

25

⧉

A Million Pieces

The next morning, I entered the foyer of Rose and John's rented home, my heart still light from the previous evening's blissful moments with Willa. Waking up beside her, seeing her beautiful face puffy and crinkled as she yawned and slowly opened her eyes, sent a surge of heat through me.

I had a feeling I would be reliving last night's events the entire day. I smiled to myself before glancing up and spotting my brother.

Randolph? What was he doing here again so soon?

Randolph paced the hallway, his entire body vibrating, exuding a sense of anxiety. My heart dropped, and my earlier bliss was replaced by a growing feeling of dread. My stomach churned.

On his turn back towards the foyer, he noticed me. His head whipped up, brows furrowed. "Anne. Where have you been?" His tone was sharp as he scolded me. "I've been worried sick."

My mind raced; I did not know how to answer. I wanted to keep the night I spent with Willa private. My chest squeezed as I gaped at my brother.

"Never mind, I don't have time for that now." Randolph waved his hand dismissively. "We're in trouble, Anne. The debt collector is calling in our family debt, and we have only days, maybe a couple of weeks at best, to pay it off."

My eyes widened, and I dropped my arms limply to my sides. "But... but I thought everything was sorted. You were starting your job as a solicitor, and we were hopeful that it would provide the means to pay off the debts."

Randolph's expression turned somber, and he sighed heavily. "Yes, I am starting as a solicitor, but the pay hasn't been confirmed yet. And even if it had been, it would take a considerable amount of time to save up the sum needed to clear all our debts. We simply don't have that luxury of time."

My heart sank as the weight of my family's dire situation settled upon me. Losing our home, our belongings, and everything my family held dear was an imminent reality. I felt a surge of desperation and frustration, struggling to comprehend why this was happening now when I had hoped to start living my own life.

"I can't believe this is happening." My voice trembled as the weight of the news settled and turned my stomach. "It's not fair, Randolph. What now?"

Randolph averted his gaze as he spoke. "I am sorry, but there is no other way... Do you have any suitors or any marriage prospects still lined up?"

"You can at least look me in the eyes when you ask me to fix our family's problem." I glared at my brother; at least he had the good sense to turn his face back toward me. "You promised me only a few days ago that I could choose to live the life that I wanted, that I did not need to marry for money." I stepped forward and smacked my hand against his chest. Randolph took a half step back. "And now, here you are, asking me to take responsibility once more. I will not; I cannot."

"Anne." Randolph's expression turned pained. "Think of Mama and Mary. Had it been just me..." He sighed, shoulders slumping. "No, if it had been only me, I would never."

"Ask it of me then. And know what I'm giving up."

"What? Anne, have you been courting someone?" Randolph sounded disapproving which only served to grate my nerves even further.

"Willa Balfour," I ground out.

"Your friend?" A flicker of surprise crossed his face though he didn't seem appalled by the notion. "You..." He swallowed, throat bobbing as he paused to gaze at me.

"Yes." My voice sounded clipped as my throat constricted.

Randolph pursed his lips and tried to lay his hand on my shoulder, but I shrugged it off. My heart broke into a million pieces while Willa's scent still lingered on my skin.

He sighed again. "Fine, if it helps. Anne, your family needs your help. Can you find a suitor to marry who can cover our debts?" He returned his hand to my shoulder. "Life isn't always fair, Anne. We must face the challenges that come our way and find a way to overcome them."

My eyes burned, turning moist as I thought of Willa and

what only minutes ago had seemed like a blissful day. I wiped at the tears spilling over, not wanting to show the depth of my grief to my brother. I had no other choice. I could not abandon my family even if...even if it meant crushing my desires and dreams. The weight of responsibility settled upon my shoulders; I had to think of a plan, a way to secure the funds needed within the limited time frame we had.

The thought of leaving Willa behind tore at my soul. I had tasted love so sweet, so passionate, that it felt like a betrayal to consider abandoning it. But the reality of my family's situation was harsh and unforgiving. Time was slipping away, and I couldn't afford to indulge in my desires when my family's future hung in the balance.

I couldn't help but feel a sense of resentment towards Randolph for placing me in this predicament. Why couldn't he have found a way to secure our financial stability before it reached such a critical point? The frustration threatened to consume me, but I knew deep down that assigning blame wouldn't solve anything.

With a heavy sigh, I resolved to push my desires aside. I couldn't let my selfishness cloud my judgment. I had a duty to my family, a duty to help secure Mary's future. I did not have the luxury of attending parties and waiting for potential suitors. Time was running out, and every moment wasted could mean losing everything my family held dear.

I closed my eyes for a moment, allowing myself a moment of sadness and longing for what could have been. Then, with a determined resolve, I pushed those emotions aside and donned the mask of the dutiful daughter and sister.

My mind raced with thoughts of Mrs. Ashbrook, the

shrewd and influential woman back in Westbridge. The idea of seeking her assistance both relieved and unsettled me. I knew that Mrs. Ashbrook's connections and wealth could expedite the process of finding a suitable husband, but it also meant relinquishing my agency in the matter.

I shared my thoughts with Randolph.

Randolph took my hands in his, his voice filled with sincerity. "Anne, I want nothing more than to see you happy. If turning to Mrs. Ashbrook is what it takes to secure our family's future, then I support your decision. But promise me this; promise me that you won't lose sight of your happiness completely. There may come a time when you find yourself with options, and I want you to choose a man who will bring you joy, not just financial stability."

My poor Randolph hadn't understood a thing about me. Not one man would bring me joy. I only wanted one thing in this world, one beautiful singular thing. Willa. And now I would never again be with her.

I swallowed thickly. "Randolph, can you prepare a carriage? I shall inform John and Rose of my decision to return to Westbridge."

Randolph nodded and stepped out the front door while I followed the hallway out back.

As I approached John and Rose in the serene back garden, the scent of blooming flowers filled the air. I had found solace in this garden, but now it seemed bittersweet.

My voice trembled as I spoke, "John, Rose, I have something important to discuss with you." Their concerned eyes met mine, urging me to continue. Taking a deep breath, I gathered my thoughts.

"I... I must return home to Westbridge." My voice tinged with regret. "Our family's situation has become even more dire, and I have no choice but to seek assistance from Mrs. Ashbrook. It pains me to leave both of you and this life in London, but our debts are pressing, and time is running out."

John's brows furrowed, his concern etched across his face. "Anne, we can't let you go back alone. We'll find a way to help; we'll—"

But I interrupted, my tone resolute. "No, John. You and Rose have already done so much for me. Sponsoring my season in London was more than I ever could have hoped for. I can't burden you any further." I did not wish to take any more charity than I had already received from the Eastons.

Rose's gaze softened, her hand reaching out to touch my arm. "But what about Willa?"

My eyes flickered with a mixture of pain and longing. I bit my lip, struggling to find the right words. "I... I can't bring Willa into this. It's too complicated, and I can't ask her to help for my family's sake. She deserves better."

Tears welled up in Rose's eyes as she embraced me, her voice choked with emotion. "Oh, Anne, you know she would —in a heartbeat."

I shook my head. "I can't. I don't want to be a burden."

Rose squeezed me tighter. "I wish there was another way. But know that we will always be here for you, and if the time comes when you need us, don't hesitate to reach out."

I nodded, my throat tightening with emotion. I cherished the bond I had formed with Rose and John, grateful for their forgiveness of my previous behavior.

As I pulled away, I forced a small smile, trying to convey

my gratitude. "Thank you, both of you, for everything. I will never forget your kindness and generosity. Please, if Willa comes here looking for me, let her know that I have no choice in this matter. It's the only way I can protect her from the burdens of our circumstances."

Rose's hand remained on my arm, her eyes filled with understanding. "We will do as you ask, Anne. Take care of yourself, and remember, love has a way of finding its destination. Don't lose hope."

With a heavy heart, I nodded, my resolve firm. I turned away from the garden and the life I had started to build in London. The weight of my duty pressed upon my shoulders, but I knew that I had to face it head-on.

26

Silence

The carriage rattled along the dusty road, its wheels creating a steady rhythm that matched the beating of my heart. Sitting across from me was my brother, Randolph, his usually composed expression marred by a hint of unease.

As the London cityscape faded into the distance, my gaze turned to the suitcases perched atop the carriage. Each one contained a piece of my past, a token of the life I was leaving behind. Amongst the folded dresses and cherished mementos, my heart ached for the absence of one particular person—Willa.

A surge of sorrow washed over me as I recalled the memory of our last moments together. I had left her without a word, without an explanation, and the weight of that decision bore heavily upon me. How could I have abandoned her, the woman I loved, without even a chance to say goodbye? It felt as if I had torn a piece of my soul away, leaving a void that threatened to swallow me whole.

Glancing at Randolph, I noticed the lines etched upon his forehead, his brows furrowed with an unspoken worry. I knew he carried his share of guilt.

His voice broke the silence, his tone laden with a mixture of concern and hesitation.

"Anne, I know this isn't what you want, and I'm sorry for the pain it causes you. But our family must find a suitable match, someone who can alleviate our debts and secure our future."

A sigh escaped my lips, my eyes drifting back to the passing scenery. I had always been a dutiful daughter, willing to sacrifice my desires for the sake of our family's well-being. Yet, as the carriage carried me further from London and from the woman who held my heart, a knot of sadness and longing formed deep within me.

"I understand, Randolph. But it doesn't make the ache any less real, the longing any less profound."

Silence settled upon us once again, the steady rhythm of the carriage wheels mirroring the contemplative thoughts swirling within my mind. I couldn't shake the weight of guilt that clung to me like a heavy cloak, nor could I silence the whispers of doubt that echoed in my soul.

Suddenly, the carriage jolted to an abrupt stop, jarring me from my thoughts and filling the air with a sense of confusion. I watched as Randolph opened the carriage door and stepped out, his voice carrying faintly through the open window as he approached the driver, seeking answers to the sudden halt.

Just as my mind began to wander, consumed by a mixture

of worry and uncertainty, a light tapping against the glass startled me. I turned my gaze towards the window, my heart skipping a beat as I laid eyes upon the unexpected visitor standing outside.

It was Willa.

My breath caught in my throat, my eyes widening with a mix of surprise and longing. How was it possible? How had she found us in this remote location on the outskirts of London? And why had she come?

Without hesitation, I opened the window, the cool breeze brushing against my face as I peered out at her. Her eyes sparkled with a mixture of relief and determination, her fiery red hair dancing in the wind.

"Anne," she whispered, her voice laced with urgency and a hint of fear. "I had to find you. I couldn't let you go without a word."

A surge of emotion washed over me, tears threatening to spill from my eyes. I had been filled with regret and longing since our abrupt parting, and now, seeing her before me, my heart felt as though it had been granted a second chance. But it couldn't be.

With a trembling hand, I reached for the door handle, my heart pounding in my chest. I stepped out of the carriage, the world around me fading into insignificance as I stood face-to-face with the woman who had captured my heart.

"I can help, Anne." The expression on her face was determined. "My father has the means to cover your family's debts. You don't have to go through this alone."

The words hung heavy in the air, Willa's offer of help mingling with the tinge of sadness that filled the space between us. Her voice held a mix of concern and frustration, her eyes searching mine for a glimmer of understanding.

I closed my eyes, feeling the weight of her words press upon my heart. The thought of relinquishing the burden that had plagued my family for far too long was tempting, but my resolve remained steadfast.

"I appreciate your offer, Willa. But this is something I must do on my own. I cannot accept your father's help."

Her eyes widened with a mixture of confusion and hurt. "But why, Anne? Why won't you let me help? Don't let your pride ruin what we have."

My voice caught in my throat, the words struggling to escape. "It's not about pride, Willa," I managed to say, my voice choking with emotion. "It's about honor, about the duty I have to my family. I cannot let them suffer any longer. And I cannot let our love be tainted by financial obligations."

Silence settled between us, the weight of our unspoken desires and conflicting emotions hanging in the air. I turned away, unable to meet her gaze, my heart aching with every step I took.

"I'm sorry, Willa." I swallowed, my voice thin. "I wish things could be different, but this is the path I must walk."

As I approached the carriage, I called to my brother; my voice tinged with a mix of determination and sadness. "Randolph, it's time to go. Please return to the carriage."

He nodded, understanding the gravity of the situation, and began to make his way back to the waiting carriage. But before we could continue our journey, Melinda stood before us, her presence a testament to the magical world that had brought us together.

I turned to face her, my brows furrowing in pain. "Melinda, please move aside. We must continue on our way." I did not know how much more I could take.

Her expression softened, her eyes filled with understanding. "Anne, I wish you the best on your journey. Remember, the bookshop will always be here for you should you ever need a place of solace."

I nodded, my heart heavy with the knowledge that I was leaving behind not only the woman I loved but also a world of enchantment and possibility. With a final glance at Willa, my voice barely rose above a whisper. "Goodbye, Willa. Know that I will always love you."

Tears welled in her eyes though she remained silent, staring at me as I walked away.

With a heavy heart, I climbed into the carriage, my gaze lingering on Willa until the very last moment.

27

For My Family's Sake

As we pulled up to our modest cottage in Westbridge, the sight of the roses climbing up its side failed to lift the heaviness in my heart. Leaving Willa behind had taken its toll on my spirit, and the weight of my family's expectations loomed large before me.

As the carriage came to a stop, I stepped out, feeling a mix of weariness and resignation. The familiar face of my younger sister, Mary, greeted us with unbridled enthusiasm. Her youthful energy brightened the gloomy cloud that had settled over me.

"Anne. Randolph." She rushed towards us with a grin from ear to ear. "Oh, how I've missed you both."

I managed a weak smile, grateful for Mary's genuine joy at our return. She was only seventeen, a sprightly and hopeful soul, yet burdened by the knowledge of the responsibilities that lay ahead for our family.

"Mary, it's good to see you too," I said, my voice tinged with weariness. "How has everything been in our absence?"

Mary beamed, her eyes sparkling with excitement. "Oh, quite eventful, I must say! But before we get into that, Mama is waiting inside. She's been working on your wedding trousseau, Anne."

My heart sank at the mention of my impending marriage, a reminder of the sacrifices I had made for my family's sake. I nodded, mustering a semblance of gratitude for my mother's efforts.

"Thank you, Mary. I should go greet Mama."

Together, Mary and I entered the cottage, the familiar scent of home comforting yet suffocating at the same time. We made our way to the parlor, where Mama sat diligently embroidering the quilt that would be part of my dowry.

"Mama," I called softly, a mix of trepidation and longing in my voice.

She looked up, her eyes lighting up with joy at the sight of us. "Anne! Randolph! You're finally home."

I approached her, a knot forming in my throat. "Yes, Mama, we're home. How have things been in our absence?"

Mama smiled, her fingers working the needle and thread. "Busy, my dear. But I've been working on something special for you." She gestured to the quilt in progress. "It will be a beautiful addition to your trousseau."

Her words struck a chord within me, a reminder of the life that awaited me—filled with expectations, obligations, and a future that had been decided for me.

I forced a smile, though it felt hollow on my lips. "Thank you, Mama. I'm sure it will be lovely."

Mary, sensing the heaviness in the air, attempted to lighten the mood. "And Mama, guess who we saw on our way here? Mr. Jacobson, the town cobbler, had a new puppy."

Mama's face lit up, momentarily distracted from the weight of my arrival. "Oh, how delightful. I do love puppies. We must visit Mr. Jacobson soon."

I took a deep breath, steeling myself for the conversation I was about to have with my mother. The weight of my unspoken desires pressed upon me, urging me to seek any glimpse of hope within the confining walls of our cottage.

"Mama," I began, my voice betraying a mix of vulnerability. "Are there... any eligible bachelors left in town? Or have they all been snatched up and set to marry?"

Mama's brow furrowed as she paused her stitching, her gaze meeting mine with a mix of sympathy and resignation. It was a question that hung heavy in the air, laden with the truth that I feared.

"Oh, my dear Anne. I'm afraid most of the eligible young men in town have indeed found their matches and have committed to a life of matrimony."

My heart sank at her words, the reality of my situation closing in around me. The limited pool of potential suitors had dwindled, leaving me with few prospects.

"But Mama, surely there must be someone, someone who's still available, someone who could see beyond the debts and the expectations?"

Mama's gaze softened, her hand reaching out to gently touch mine. "Oh, my dear child, I wish it were so. But in a town as small as ours, where everyone knows everyone else's business, the choices become limited, and the families have already made their arrangements."

A wave of resignation washed over me, and I averted my gaze. I truly had no other choice then; I would need to speak with Mrs. Ashbrook.

"I understand, Mama. Thank you for being honest with me."

As I made my way back outside to retrieve my luggage, the lighthearted banter between Randolph and Mary continued, their laughter echoing through the air. I couldn't help but crack a small smile at their attempts to lighten the mood, grateful for their efforts even though my heart still felt heavy.

With a sigh, I reached for my suitcases, their weight serving as a tangible reminder of the life I had left behind in London. As I carried them back into the house, I couldn't help but feel a sense of anticipation mingled with apprehension about the upcoming meeting with Mrs. Ashbrook.

Upon entering my bedroom, I placed my suitcases on the floor and took a moment to glance around the familiar space. The sun streamed through the lace curtains, casting a soft glow on the worn wooden furniture and floral wallpaper. It was a sanctuary of sorts, a place where I could retreat and gather my thoughts.

I quickly shed my travel-worn attire, selecting a clean dress from my wardrobe. As I slipped it over my head, the soft fabric cascading down around me, I felt a small spark of rejuvenation. It may not have been the grandest of garments, but it was a small act of self-care, a way to ready myself for the meeting ahead.

I smoothed out the wrinkles with delicate hands, my

reflection in the mirror reflecting a mix of determination and uncertainty. It was time to face the world with grace, to present myself as a suitable match for Mrs. Ashbrook's groom of choice. The weight of societal expectations bore down upon me, urging me to conform and put aside my desires for the sake of my family's well-being.

With a final adjustment to my appearance, I took a steadying breath and made my way downstairs, ready to face whatever lay ahead.

When I returned to the sitting room, Randolph appraised my freshened state of dress. "You intend to visit Mrs. Ashbrook today?"

Randolph's question pulled me from my thoughts, and I turned to face him, a determined expression on my face. "Yes, Randolph. I intend to pay a visit to Mrs. Ashbrook right away. There's no time like the present."

Mama's gaze shifted from her embroidery to meet mine, a mixture of concern and pride in her eyes. "Are you ready for this, my dear Anne?"

I took a deep breath, summoning the courage within me. "Yes, Mama. I am ready. I will face this meeting with Mrs. Ashbrook head-on and present myself as the best match for whomever she offers up."

Mama's eyes softened, and she reached out to gently squeeze my hand. "I am proud of you, Anne. You have shown great strength and resilience in the face of our family's circumstances. If only your poor papa..." Mama sighed. "If he had known, I doubt he would ever have left us like this."

I smiled at her words, the weight of her approval offering me a sense of reassurance. Turning my attention back to

Randolph, I made a small request. "Randolph, would it be possible for you to take me in our curricle?"

Randolph's eyes sparkled with a mix of mischief and understanding. "Of course, Anne." A mischievous grin tugged at the corners of his mouth. "A ride in our curricle it is. We shall make our entrance in style."

"I venture it is more appreciated than me arriving covered in dirt from a horseback ride," I quipped back.

While Randolph prepared the curricle, my stomach dropped as a chill ran through my body. I wished I could hide, but I had to go on. This was for my family.

I glanced back at Mama and Mary, their loving gazes following me. With a determined smile, I assured them. "I will do my best, Mama."

As I climbed into the curricle beside Randolph, the carriage swayed, signaling the beginning of a new chapter in my life. With my heart brimming with determination, I set off on another journey. This time toward Mrs. Ashbrook's estate, ready to face whatever lay ahead.

28

Mrs. Ashbrook

As the butler announced my arrival, I took a moment to gather my composure before stepping into the elegant drawing room of Mrs. Ashbrook's estate. The room exuded an air of refinement and sophistication, its walls adorned with exquisite paintings and the soft glow of sunlight streaming through the windows.

Mrs. Ashbrook, a woman of regal stature and poise, sat gracefully in a high-backed chair, her eyes fixed upon me as I entered. Her raised hand signaled for me to approach her, and I carefully made my way toward her, feeling a mix of nervousness and determination.

"Miss Blakeley, what a surprise," Mrs. Ashbrook greeted me with a polite smile. "I assumed you were in London, attending the marriage mart. You were being sponsored by the Eastons, were you not?"

I inclined my head respectfully, meeting her gaze with

sincerity. "Indeed, Mrs. Ashbrook, circumstances have taken an unexpected turn for my family. Our financial situation has declined, and it is not feasible for me to partake in the London marriage mart anymore."

Mrs. Ashbrook's eyes softened with understanding, her gaze searching my face for any signs of desperation or deceit. With a graceful gesture, she motioned for me to take a seat opposite her. I settled into the plush chair, my hands folded neatly in my lap, and took a steadying breath.

"I must be honest with you, Mrs. Ashbrook. I have come here today to ask for your assistance. I need a suitor who can overlook my family's unfortunate debts and help us in resolving them."

Mrs. Ashbrook's expression remained composed, but her eyes glimmered with curiosity. "Go on, Miss Blakeley."

I took a moment to gather my thoughts, then continued, my voice filled with genuine honesty. "I understand that this is an unconventional request, but my intentions are true. I am searching for a partner who can see past the financial burdens my family carries, someone who can offer stability and security. If you would be so kind, Mrs. Ashbrook, I ask for your guidance and assistance in finding such a suitor."

A silence hung in the air as Mrs. Ashbrook contemplated my words. Her eyes studied my face, assessing my sincerity. Finally, she nodded slowly, her expression softening.

"Miss Blakeley, I appreciate your candor." Her tone carried a mixture of compassion and pragmatism. "Your situation is not an easy one, but I commend you for your honesty. Rest assured, I will do my best to assist you in finding a suitor who can meet your requirements. Could you please provide me with more details about the extent of your family's debt? How dire is the situation, and how soon do we need to arrange a marriage?"

I took a deep breath, steeling myself for the reality of the situation. "Mrs. Ashbrook, the situation is indeed quite dire. Our debts amount to a substantial sum, and the creditors have given us a deadline. We have, at most, a few weeks before the debt must be settled. At worst, we have mere days."

A flicker of concern passed over Mrs. Ashbrook's features, her brow furrowing slightly. She was well aware of the challenges posed by such a constrained timeline. I continued, trying to maintain a sense of optimism amidst the uncertainty.

"I understand the gravity of the task at hand, Mrs. Ashbrook. While I do not wish to rush into marriage, I am prepared to make certain compromises to secure my family's financial future. Time is of the essence, and I am willing to explore potential matches with earnest consideration."

Mrs. Ashbrook nodded sympathetically, her eyes conveying her understanding of the weight on my shoulders. "Miss Blakeley, I appreciate your honesty and the sacrifices you are willing to make for the sake of your family. Rest assured; I will do everything in my power to expedite this process and find a suitable match within the given time frame. You are not alone in this endeavor."

She pressed a finger against her pursed lips as she considered something. "I have a few possible matches I am thinking of. Mind you, none will be as outstanding a match as could be found at the marriage mart. But, I suppose we shouldn't be bothered by that now."

I flinched, then nodded in agreement after smoothing my face back into what I hoped looked like a grateful smile.

"Yes," Mrs. Ashbrook continued. "I shall send out letters to a few of my acquaintances. I'll have my foot servant deliver them today. How about we meet up again tomorrow, say teatime?" She sniffed and gazed back at me, her posture as rigid as ever. "Come dressed in your finest day attire."

I curtsied. "Thank you, Mrs. Ashbrook."

"You are welcome, my dear." Mrs. Ashbrook motioned at the butler. "Let us get you married. Here, I'll have Rupert show you out."

***

As I entered the elegant salon, a flutter of nerves danced in my stomach. Mrs. Ashbrook, seated at the table surrounded by three other women, beckoned me forward with a warm smile. I took a deep breath, summoning all the grace and composure I could muster, and glided towards them.

The room was filled with the delicate aroma of freshly brewed tea, mingling with the sweet scent of pastries and the soft murmur of conversation. The women turned their attention toward me, their eyes filled with curiosity and anticipation. I reminded myself to hold my head high and radiate confidence, despite the nervous flutter in my heart.

As I approached the table, the butler pulled out a chair for me, and I took my seat beside Mrs. Ashbrook. The other women, whom I presumed to be the mothers of the prospective suitors, offered polite smiles, their eyes scrutinizing me with a mix of interest and assessment.

I glanced down at the spread of delicacies before me, a tempting array of pastries and dainty finger sandwiches. I reached for a delicate porcelain teacup and poured myself a cup of fragrant tea, allowing the warmth to soothe my racing thoughts.

Mrs. Ashbrook, ever the gracious hostess, introduced me to the other ladies seated around the table. Each mother smiled politely and extended a hand for a brief handshake. I reciprocated with polite greetings, hoping to make a favorable impression.

As I sipped my tea, I observed the women, trying to gauge their demeanor and discern any hints about their sons who might be potential suitors. It was a delicate dance, this mingling of personalities and the unspoken negotiations of courtship.

The conversation flowed, mostly centered around the pleasantness of the day and the beauty of the estate. I listened attentively, contributing when appropriate, all the while conscious of the importance of making a favorable impression. I couldn't help but feel a mix of excitement and trepidation, knowing that the fate of my family's financial future hinged on the outcome of these meetings.

During the conversation, my gaze caught Mrs. Ashbrook's eyes, and she subtly nodded toward the tray of pastries. Taking the cue, I delicately selected a dainty éclair and began to savor its sweet cream filling. The taste was a welcome distraction, a fleeting moment of pleasure amidst the weighty matters at hand.

As Mrs. Ashbrook announced her plan for a gathering that evening, a surge of anticipation coursed through me. I sat upright in my chair, my heart quickening with both excitement and a hint of nervousness. This would be my opportunity to meet the prospective suitors, gauge their characters, and determine if any of them held the potential to be my future husband.

Mrs. Ashbrook's voice carried a firm but elegant tone as she addressed the mothers seated around the table. She emphasized the importance of the gathering, explaining that it would provide an occasion for me to get to know the young men in a relaxed and informal setting. My heart skipped a beat at the thought of meeting them, my mind already swirling with questions and worries.

As Mrs. Ashbrook concluded her remarks, the mothers nodded in agreement and began discussing logistics and arrangements. I listened intently, trying to absorb every detail.

Mrs. Ashbrook turned her attention to me, her eyes filled with a mix of kindness and encouragement. "I assure you that this gathering will allow ample opportunity for conversation and connection. I urge you to approach the evening with an open mind and a genuine desire to get to know each suitor."

29

⚬⚬⚬

Selecting A Suitor

As the evening sun cast its golden glow through the tall windows of the ballroom, illuminating the polished parquet floor, I stood alongside Mrs. Ashbrook, my gaze drifting beyond the room to the beckoning doors that led to the back garden. The music troupe's soft melodies floated in the air, creating an enchanting ambiance that mingled with the hum of anticipation.

One by one, the suitors and their mothers entered the ballroom, their names announced with a flourish, along with other guests to fill the dance floor. Mrs. Ashbrook welcomed them graciously, introducing me as Anne Blakeley. With each polite exchange, I offered a smile and kind words, acknowledging their presence.

Yet, as I engaged in small talk, my mind couldn't help but wander to thoughts of Willa. Memories of her infectious laughter and the way her eyes sparkled with mischief flooded my thoughts, contrasting with the current atmosphere. The weight of regret began to seep in, knowing that I had left her behind without a proper explanation or a chance for us to be together.

Amidst the introductions, a suitor stepped forward, extending his hand and asking for the honor of our first dance. I accepted with a polite nod, masking my inner reluctance. As we joined the other couples on the dance floor, my feet gracefully moved in time with the music while my mind grappled with conflicting emotions.

"Henry Everton," the first suitor reminded me.

A polite smile adorned my lips, concealing the thoughts that lingered in the recesses of my mind. "Glad to make your acquaintance." The music swelled around us, its gentle rhythm guiding our steps as we moved in sync.

Mr. Everton, a tall and reserved gentleman, engaged me in conversation as we glided across the floor. Our discussion turned to our respective hobbies and interests, an attempt to unearth the shared passions that could potentially forge a connection.

"I must admit, Miss Blakeley, I find great solace in the art of painting," Mr. Everton confided, his eyes flickering with a hint of enthusiasm. "Capturing the world's beauty on canvas brings me immeasurable joy."

I listened with rapt attention, appreciating his dedication to the arts. "How wonderful. Art possesses the power to evoke emotions and transport us to different realms. I, too, have a deep appreciation for creative pursuits."

His curiosity piqued, Mr. Everton inquired further, "And

may I ask, Miss Blakeley, what art form brings you the greatest delight?"

A soft sigh escaped my lips, a fleeting yearning for the pianoforte that stood regally in the parlor of our family's cottage. "Music, particularly playing the pianoforte, is a passion of mine. The keys beneath my fingers, the melody cascading through the air—there's something magical about bringing music to life."

Mr. Everton's gaze brightened, a spark of shared enthusiasm igniting between us. "How delightful! I must admit I find great pleasure in attending musical performances. Perhaps, in the future, we could attend a concert together?"

I considered his proposal, appreciating his genuine interest. While his presence held an air of stability and respectability, my heart couldn't help but yearn for the spontaneous laughter and infectious joy that Willa had brought into my life. Still, I needed to remain open to the possibilities that lay ahead.

"That sounds lovely, Mr. Everton. I appreciate your fondness for the arts, and I would be delighted to share that experience with you."

As the dance continued, we conversed further, exploring our hopes, dreams, and desires. While Mr. Everton possessed many admirable qualities, I couldn't shake the lingering sense that something was missing, a connection that I had once known and cherished.

Our dance drew to a close, and with a polite curtsy, I expressed my gratitude. Mr. Everton returned the gesture, his eyes holding a glimmer of hope.

"Thank you for the dance, Miss Blakeley. I look forward

to our future conversations and discovering more about who you are."

A soft smile graced my lips. "The pleasure is mine, Mr. Everton. I am grateful for the opportunity to get to know you better."

As Mr. Henry Everton returned me to the side of Mrs. Ashbrook, I readied myself for the next dance partner who awaited me. Little did I know that this encounter would be quite different from the pleasant conversation and easy movements I had just experienced.

The second suitor, Mr. Charles Hargrove, approached with an air of self-assurance that bordered on arrogance. His manners lacked refinement, evident in the curt nod he offered instead of an elegant bow. With an apologetic smile directed at Mrs. Ashbrook, I took his outstretched hand, steeling myself for what awaited me on the dance floor.

As the music began to play, Mr. Hargrove's lack of grace became painfully apparent. His movements were clumsy, and his footwork, quite frankly, atrocious. I stumbled to maintain the rhythm, silently cursing my misfortune at being paired with someone more interested in showing off his own supposed skills rather than engaging in the dance.

His conversation was as uninspiring as his dancing, veering into topics of little substance and laden with crude remarks. My attempts at redirecting the conversation to more meaningful matters were met with dismissive grunts and condescending smirks. It became clear that Mr. Hargrove's interests lay in shallow pursuits, leaving me disheartened.

Throughout the dance, I struggled to maintain a polite facade, though my patience waned with each passing minute.

The once enchanting ballroom now felt suffocating, its walls seemingly closing in on me as I yearned for an escape from Mr. Hargrove's company.

Finally, the dance came to an end, and I swiftly withdrew my hand from his grasp, offering a forced smile that did not do much to conceal my relief. Mr. Hargrove, oblivious to the discomfort he had caused, simply nodded and moved on to a different dance partner.

As I regained my composure, a mix of emotions swirled within me. Disappointment, certainly, for the lackluster encounter I had just endured. Yet, beneath it all, there remained a glimmer of determination—a reminder that quitting was not an option.

With renewed resolve, I composed myself and directed my gaze towards the last suitor, hoping that amidst the three possibilities, there might be one whose company would rekindle the spark of excitement and authenticity that had once defined my experiences with Willa.

I took a deep breath as I stepped away from the crowded ballroom and made my way to the refreshments table. The lively music and conversations had started to overwhelm me, and I needed a moment of respite to collect my thoughts. I poured myself a glass of refreshing lemonade and sipped it, letting its coolness soothe my nerves.

Lost in contemplation, I was startled when a voice interrupted my thoughts. I turned to find Mr. Edward Sinclair, the third suitor, standing beside me. His expression seemed detached, as if his mind was elsewhere, and it was evident that he was not particularly interested in our conversation.

He asked the obligatory questions about my family, but his lack of engagement was palpable.

"Why are you here?" I asked, hoping to cut through his facade.

He hesitated, his back straightening as his gaze swept across me in contemplation. He must have thought it wise to answer the truth. "I must confess that my mother is the driving force behind this. She's desperate to get her hands on some grandchildren."

"And what is it that you are looking for?"

Finally, a smile broke through his uninterested appearance. "I yearn to travel." He shrugged a bit sheepishly. "Perhaps I'll join a militia, follow them to every corner of Britain. That has always seemed like a good career choice to me—away from my rather stifling mother and out on the open roads, blue skies above me."

Though I couldn't bring myself to express it aloud, I shared in his desire for freedom and the yearning to pursue one's passions. The weight of societal obligations and the pressure to conform weighed heavily on both of us.

At that moment, I felt a surge of compassion for Mr. Edward Sinclair. We were both trapped in a web of expectations and obligations, longing for a life that felt authentic. But amidst our shared understanding, my heart yearned for someone else—the one person who understood me and made me feel alive. Willa.

As I listened to the third suitor, my gaze wandered across the ballroom, catching glimpses of other couples immersed in their conversations and laughter. The contrast between the dullness of the present moment and the vibrancy that Willa had brought to my life grew starker with each passing second.

I couldn't help but compare the suitor's company to the laughter and the shared adventures I had experienced with Willa. Willa had always managed to make me smile, to fill my heart with a sense of exhilaration. The realization of what I had left behind, what I might be sacrificing, began to weigh upon me.

Adding a quick curtsy, I excused myself from Mr. Sinclair's side. There were no good choices, but still, one had to be made.

As I returned to Mrs. Ashbrook's side, her expectant gaze met mine. It was clear that she was eager to hear my thoughts on the suitors and if any of them had managed to capture my interest. Taking a deep breath, I mustered a polite smile and prepared myself to deliver my decision.

"Well, Mrs. Ashbrook," I began, choosing my words, "after speaking with each suitor, I have given the matter considerable thought. While none of them ignited a spark within me, if I must choose, I believe the first suitor would be the best option."

Mrs. Ashbrook's eyebrows raised, betraying her surprise. She had likely anticipated a more enthusiastic response from me, but alas, the connection I yearned for remained absent. Still, I needed to make a practical choice for the sake of my family's financial future.

"I understand your consideration, Miss Blakeley," Mrs. Ashbrook replied with a nod. "Rest assured, I will arrange everything with the suitor's mother. We shall proceed with the necessary formalities and make the necessary arrangements."

Her words were filled with a sense of finality, and while I appreciated her efforts, a tinge of melancholy lingered within me. This decision was not borne out of love or genuine affection but rather out of duty and the pressing need to secure my family's well-being.

With a heavy heart, I braced myself for the path that lay ahead, knowing that it would be a journey devoid of true passion and heartfelt connection.

30

The Chapel

Three days had passed since I had chosen the man I was going to marry. Mr. Everton—Henry—my soon-to-be husband. I tasted his name but found nothing but ash in my throat. I sat in front of my bedroom mirror, my gaze fixed upon the reflection staring back at me; I couldn't help but feel an overwhelming sense of strangeness. The wedding dress I wore felt like a costume, as if it belonged to someone else entirely. It wasn't me that I saw; it was a version of myself molded and shaped by societal expectations and familial obligations.

Dread began to coil within me, tightening its grip on my heart. The questions started to flood my mind, cascading like a relentless stream. Should I go through with this wedding? Had I given up on Willa too quickly, dismissing the love we shared? Was my pride a barrier that prevented me from accepting her offer of help? Doubt, like a relentless companion, whispered in my ear, urging me to reconsider.

But as I gazed at the reflection before me, I was reminded of the weight of my family's expectations. Their financial burdens rested heavily upon my shoulders, and at this moment, it seemed as if the entire fate of my loved ones hinged upon my decision. How could I let them down now when they needed me most? The responsibility felt suffocating, tugging at my conscience.

Torn between the love I once shared with Willa and the duty I owed my family, I battled with my emotions. Should I sacrifice my happiness for the sake of others? Was there a way to find a balance, to fulfill my obligations while still holding on to the love that had ignited a flame within me?

My shoulders sank. It seemed not.

"Anne, my dear. Are you ready?" My mother peeked around the corner. "Randolph has readied the carriage; we are to set out soon."

I let out a puff of air and then forced a smile upon my face. I turned to face my mama. "I am ready; let us head to the chapel. Is Mary already waiting for us?"

"She is. We are all ready for you."

As we made our way to the small chapel, the weight of the world seemed to rest upon my shoulders. We stopped the carriage at the bottom of the hill and continued on foot. Beside me, Randolph walked with a supportive presence, his steady stride matching my own. My dear mama, her eyes filled with both joy and concern, walked beside us, her love emanating from every fiber of her being. And Mary, my sweet younger sister, handed me a small bouquet of roses she had crafted from our garden. The delicate petals carried the fragrance of home, a comforting reminder amidst the whirlwind of emotions.

Approaching the chapel, its humble façade stood as a beacon of familiarity in a sea of uncertainty. The stone walls echoed with the laughter and prayers of countless Westbridge residents, who had gathered here for Christmas celebrations and sermons over the years. Now, it would bear witness to a different kind of ceremony, one that would forever alter the course of my life.

Inside, the air was crisp, carrying the anticipation that filled the hearts of those gathered. The flickering candles cast a warm glow upon the wooden pews, and the familiar scent of aged wood mingled with the fragrance of my modest bouquet. Mr. Willoughby, as thin and greasy looking as always, stood at the altar, ready to guide us through this ill-fated union.

I took a moment to steal a glance at my family, their presence providing both solace and strength. Mama's eyes shimmered with unshed tears, a testament to the love and hope she held for my future. Randolph, though burdened with his own guilt and regrets, offered me a reassuring smile, encouraging me to follow the path I had chosen. And Mary, my dear sister, her face glowing with youthful innocence, whispered words of support that touched my heart.

Mary always meant well. Perhaps we had kept her too sheltered, too protected because even now, she seemed to have no idea that I was merely going through with this for her and our family's sake.

Near the front of the altar, my soon-to-be-husband stood and faced the entrance. He looked solemn as he nodded his head at me. Neither of us expected a love match.

Clutching the bouquet in my trembling hands, the weight of the moment threatened to consume me. The absence of my dear papa, who should have been here by my side, was a constant ache in my heart despite his actions leading me here. But Randolph, my steadfast brother, stood in his place, his arm linking with mine, providing a semblance of strength.

Randolph's voice, barely above a whisper, reached my ears.

"Thank you, Anne. I can never repay you for what you are doing today. Our debt should not have been yours to bear, but I am ever so grateful that you are helping us."

I nodded, my gaze meeting his, acknowledging the complexity of our situation. We had trodden a difficult path, making choices that carried consequences, both intended and unforeseen.

With a gentle squeeze of my arm, Randolph released his grip and found his seat among our family in the pew. I watched him retreat, a mixture of emotions playing across his face. The weight of responsibility he carried for our family's well-being was etched into the lines on his forehead, his eyes filled with a blend of pride, regret, and care for me.

As Mr. Everton, my soon-to-be husband, stood before me, his gaze locked onto mine; I tried to muster a sense of resolve. We had embarked on this journey together, bound by the decisions made for our families. But as the wedding ceremony began, led by the vicar, Mr. Willoughby, an unsettling unease started building within me.

Mr. Willoughby, the greasy-looking vicar, emanated an air of insincerity. His voice carried a hollow tone as he recited the familiar vows, his eyes darting around the chapel as if searching for something. I shifted uncomfortably, feeling a sense of disquietude grow within me.

But just as the ceremony was reaching its crescendo, a disruption shattered the solemnity of the chapel. A voice, strong and filled with desperation, echoed through the sacred space, commanding everyone's attention. My heart skipped a beat as I turned to see Willa, her figure framed in the doorway, her eyes filled with an intensity that matched the fervor in her voice.

"Stop the wedding." Her voice pierced through the hushed atmosphere. The world around me seemed to freeze, time standing still in that moment of shock and disbelief. Gasps of surprise filled the air, and all eyes turned to Willa, her presence disrupting the carefully choreographed proceedings.

Confusion and anticipation swirled within me as I locked eyes with Willa, our connection unbroken despite the chaos unfolding around us. The weight of her words hung heavy in the air, stirring a whirlwind of emotions within me. Doubts, regrets, and a flood of memories surged to the surface, threatening to overwhelm me.

I found myself torn between the obligations I had shouldered and the desires that whispered in the depths of my heart.

I stood, frozen in shock, as Melinda and the marquis followed Willa into the chapel. My heart raced, my mind a whirlwind of confusion and conflicting emotions. Without a second thought, I rushed forward, reaching out to grasp Willa's arm and pulling her with me in a hasty retreat from the chapel. We passed by Melinda and her father, their presence a blur as my focus narrowed solely on Willa.

Once outside, the cool air embraced us, providing a momentary respite from the intensity of the situation. My breathing turned shallow and thin, and my skin prickled. I turned to face Willa, my voice trembling.

"Willa, what are you doing here?" My eyes searched hers for clarification.

Willa frowned, her posture rigid as she pursed her lips. "I'm here to stop you from making a mistake." She shook her head, lifting her hands toward me. "I cannot let you marry some man you've barely met. Not when I love you." She breathed, her chest falling. "And you love me, I know you do. I've seen it; I've felt it. You have told me so in your own words. How could you bear to leave me in London? We could have everything we ever wanted. It is all right there within our grasp."

Her eyes bore into mine, searching for any sign of reciprocation. The weight of her emotions, laid bare before me, filled the space between us with a fragile tension. I felt my breath catch, a mixture of surprise, fear, and an unfathomable longing stirring within me.

The realization dawned upon me, and I could no longer deny the truth that had been silently growing within my own heart. Willa, with her infectious spirit and undeniable presence, had woven herself into the fabric of my being. She had become an integral part of my thoughts, my dreams, my desires.

Tears welled up in my eyes as I reached out, gently cupping her face in my hands. "Willa," I whispered, my voice trembling with a mix of emotions. "I never thought... I never allowed myself to believe... but I can't deny it any longer. I have been a fool to turn you away. You've had my heart in a vice from the moment I saw you in that dress shop trying to find the ugliest dress possible. I love you. My pride be damned."

"You're an idiot, Anne." Tears spilled across Willa's cheeks, and she kissed me hard, lips crushing against mine. I welcomed the twinge of pain.

I agreed I had been an idiot. "I have been prideful, I've been stupid, and I can't deny that I've been unable to stop thinking about you, Willa."

The walls I had erected to protect myself crumbled, leaving me exposed and vulnerable. My heart ached with the recognition of the love I had denied, the connection I had tried to bury. But now, standing face to face with Willa, I couldn't ignore the truth.

"Is it too late, Willa? Can we still find our happiness together, despite the mistakes I've made? Can I take you up on your offer to help my family?"

The answer hung in the air, the outcome uncertain. But I knew that I was willing to fight for Willa, for the love that had blossomed between us. I was ready to embrace a future where pride took a backseat to the longing of my heart.

Willa sighed as she embraced me, pressing her lips against my ear. "Oh, Anne, of course. You never need to ask for I will always take care of you. I shall consider it my duty from this day forward. Always."

31

Accounts Settled

I strode into the chapel, my heart pounding in my chest as the weight of my decision settled upon me. The air was thick with tension, and all eyes were on me. Mrs. Ashbrook, sitting at the front pew, wore an amused expression as if she had expected something like this all along. Mr. Willoughby, the vicar, stood beside her, his thin and greasy figure looking displeased.

Stopping about halfway down the aisle, I sucked in a breath. I needed to get the words out now. "I am breaking off the wedding." My voice echoed through the chapel, and a loud silence hung across the guests. Small murmurings could be heard, but I ignored them.

The vicar cleared his throat; his discontent was evident in his voice. "Miss Blakeley, this is highly unconventional and rather rude, I must say. It is not proper to call off a wedding in such a manner. Think of your holy matrimony, the vow you are making in front of your god. Can you shirk your duties and leave your groom-to-be like this?"

Before he could continue, Randolph, my dear brother, stepped forward and firmly placed a hand on the vicar's shoulder, guiding him to sit down on a nearby pew. I couldn't help but feel a sense of gratitude towards Randolph for intervening.

Mama looked at me with a mixture of confusion and concern. "Anne, what are you doing?"

Taking another deep breath, I walked towards her, the weight of my decision heavy upon my shoulders. "Mother, I am doing what I should have done a long time ago. I am swallowing my pride and accepting help when it is offered. I am choosing to do what makes me happy."

Her eyes softened as she realized the depth of my conviction. "But, Anne—"

Interrupting her, I reached out and took her hand. "Mother, trust me. Everything will be sorted. We will find our way."

Turning to face Mr. Henry Everton, my almost-groom, I felt a pang of guilt for the disruption I had caused. I approached him with a mixture of apprehension and apology. "Mr. Everton, I am deeply sorry for what is happening. It was unfair of me to continue with a wedding when my heart belongs to another."

To my surprise, he smiled kindly at me, his eyes reflecting a sense of understanding. "Miss Blakeley, love cannot be forced. I appreciate your honesty, and I wish you nothing but happiness."

As the weight of the moment began to lift, a sense of relief washed over me. I had chosen my path, following the call of my heart, and though the road ahead might be uncertain, I wouldn't be walking it alone. I would be with Willa.

I glanced over to where Willa stood, my heart beating a loud march. I did not know where the future would lead, but I wanted to know desperately.

I hurried over to my family and approached Randolph, taking hold of his arm and guiding him back to where Willa and her father stood. There was only one thing left to do before I could start my life with Willa. I wanted my worrying to end.

"Randolph, we need your help." I stared up at my brother with raised brows. "Tell us, where can we find the creditor?"

Randolph's eyes met mine, nodding as he considered my request. "He has an office in Bath."

"Bath?" My mind was racing with thoughts of the long journey that lay before us. "Why would Father have dealings with a creditor who operates at such a distant location?"

Randolph scrunched up as he stared at his boots. "I believe Father intended to keep the debt hidden from his peers. He must have thought that locating the creditor far away would reduce the chances of the news spreading."

The Marquis of Bambreich, ever the astute observer, interjected with a question. "Is time of the essence, Randolph? How urgent is this matter?"

Randolph's expression grew graver. "Time is of the utmost importance. The more we delay, the more complicated the situation may become. We must confront my father's creditor. Proceedings to take possession of our home and belongings have been started already."

The marquis nodded. "Then we shall waste no more time. We must make haste to Bath and face this challenge head-on."

I felt a surge of gratitude for the marquis' support and Willa's unwavering presence by my side. "I want to go as well."

Willa, her eyes brimming with unwavering love and support, squeezed my hand. "I want to be there for you, Anne. We will face this challenge together, just as we have faced everything else."

Melinda, always eager for an adventure, stepped forward, her eyes shining with determination. "Count me in too. I won't let you travel all that way alone." She grasped the marquis' hand.

The marquis' gaze shifted to Melinda, a knowing smile gracing his lips. "I would not have it any other way, Melinda."

***

The rhythmic clip-clop of the horses' hooves echoed in my ears as the carriage pressed forward, carrying us closer to Bath. The journey had been long and wearisome, the road rugged and unforgiving, but our spirits remained unyielding. Three days and two nights had passed since we left our familiar surroundings, spending restless nights in roadside inns as we pressed on toward our destination.

Now, Bath lay before us, its grandeur evident even from a distance. The River Avon meandered through the city, surrounded by picturesque hills that added to its natural splendor. I couldn't help but feel a mix of anticipation and trepidation as we approached the city that held the answers we sought.

As the carriage came to a halt, I peered out the window, taking in the sights and sounds of the bustling city. The air was alive with the energy of the people going about their daily lives. It was a stark contrast to the somber atmosphere we had left behind at the chapel.

The marquis, ever the considerate gentleman, turned to our weary group, his voice filled with concern. "Perhaps you all need some time to freshen up and rest before we proceed with our purpose?"

I exchanged a glance with Willa, conveying my eagerness to confront the creditor and settle the debt once and for all. "Thank you, Marquis, but I would prefer to visit the creditor as soon as possible. We have come this far, and I don't wish to delay any further."

Willa nodded in agreement. "Anne is right. Let us face this challenge head-on and bring an end to this debt that has haunted her family for far too long."

Melinda chimed in with a mischievous grin. "I'm ready for some action! Let's go and give this creditor a run for their money!"

The marquis gave a nod of approval. "Very well. Let us proceed and seek the resolution we have journeyed so far to find."

With renewed determination and a sense of purpose, we stepped out of the carriage onto the streets of Bath. The city, with its elegant architecture and vibrant atmosphere, welcomed our presence. We traversed the bustling streets, our footsteps resolute.

Soon, we found ourselves standing before the creditor's place of business, the door beckoning us forward. I took a deep breath, wiping my palms on my dress. We stepped into the building, the heavy scent of ink and paper filling the air. The sound of shuffling papers and the occasional clink of coins echoed through the room. Randolph took the lead.

"Excuse me," Randolph addressed a worker who was occupied behind a desk, diligently running numbers. "Is Mr. Harrington available? We need to speak with him urgently."

The worker looked up, his eyes red from hours of poring over calculations. He adjusted his spectacles and glanced at us, taking in our determined faces. "Mr. Harrington? Yes, he is upstairs in his office. You'll find him on the second floor."

"Thank you," I said, gratitude lacing my voice.

We made our way up the creaking wooden staircase, the steps worn down by countless visitors seeking solutions to their financial troubles. Each floor passed in a blur as anticipation coursed through my veins. We were determined to settle the debt and free ourselves from its grasp.

Finally, we arrived at the second floor, where the hallway stretched before us, lined with closed doors. We scanned the brass plaques affixed to each one, searching for the name we sought. And there it was, gleaming in golden letters, Mr. Arthur Harrington.

Taking a deep breath, I reached for the door handle, feeling the cool metal beneath my fingertips. The room beyond held the answers we needed, the key to our liberation from the suffocating weight of debt. With a glance at Willa, Randolph, Melinda, and the marquis, I pushed open the door.

Inside, Mr. Harrington sat behind a well-organized desk surrounded by stacks of documents and ledgers. His sharp eyes met ours as we entered, his head cocking to one side as he crossed his arms. He straightened in his chair, ready to address our presence.

"Good day, Mr. Harrington," Randolph said, his voice steady. "We have come to discuss a matter of utmost importance. We wish to settle a debt and seek a resolution."

Mr. Harrington's expression softened slightly, his professional facade giving way to curiosity. "Ah, I see. Please, have a seat. Let us discuss the details of your case."

We remained standing as Mr. Harrington offered seats to our small group, the lack of available chairs evident. Willa, Melinda, and I exchanged glances, agreeing to remain on our feet.

Randolph and the marquis took the two available seats, their postures radiating a sense of confidence.

The creditor rested his arms on the desk. "And who do I have the pleasure of speaking with today?"

"I am Mr. Randolph Blakeley," my brother introduced himself with a polite nod. "And this is my companion, the Marquis of Bambreich."

Mr. Harrington's gaze sharpened as he leaned forward. It was clear that the mention of the marquis' title had piqued his curiosity, perhaps even presented an opportunity that he had not anticipated.

"It is a pleasure to meet you, Mr. Blakeley and Marquis." Mr. Harrington's tone carried a touch of deference. "How may I assist such distinguished guests today?"

The gravity of our purpose and the potential influence of the marquis' presence in this negotiation seemed to hang in the air, raising the stakes of our encounter. We had come prepared, armed with determination and resolve, but now, with the unexpected advantage of the marquis' status, our chances of finding a favorable resolution appeared to be even greater.

Randolph cleared his throat, assuming the role of our spokesperson. "We have come to discuss a debt that has been weighing on our family for some time. We are prepared to settle the amount owed and seek a fair agreement to resolve this matter."

Mr. Harrington raised his eyebrows, his attention now focused on Randolph's words. The weight of his gaze seemed to emphasize the importance of our plea, as if he understood that our futures hung in the balance.

"I see," Mr. Harrington said, his voice tinged with anticipation. "If you would kindly provide me with the details of the debt, we can proceed with finding a mutually agreeable solution."

"My father, the late Mr. Blakeley, took out numerous lines of credit through your office. You have started proceedings to claim our belongings as repayment."

"Blakeley...Blakeley...Ah, yes." The creditor straightened as if the answer had come to him in a sudden wave of knowledge. "I am aware of your situation. Now... have you come to settle his debts?" The creditor looked at my brother with a plain-faced expression.

"I have," the marquis interjected. He pulled banknotes from his inner jacket pocket and slapped them on the desk. "I trust that these are enough to settle any debts?" He lifted his brow as he waited for an answer.

The creditor picked up the banknotes and thumbed through them, licking his lips as he counted. "Yes, I say this will do nicely."

"Can I have the contract my father signed returned to me?" Randolph held out his hand, snapping the creditor out of his musings.

"Yes, just a moment." The creditor stood, stuffing the bank notes inside his breast pocket, and walked to a file cabinet. After a few moments, he returned to his seat with a signed contract, handing it to Randolph. "This is it."

"That is all? No other debts or contracts?" Randolph grasped the contract, staring at it as if it might jump up and bite him.

"That is it," the creditor confirmed. "We no longer have business together."

All our moods were lifted once we exited the building.

"It is all over." Randolph sighed and turned to the marquis, grasping his hand and shaking it. "Thank you for your help. I do not know how I can repay you."

The marquis smiled, his eyes flitting to Willa for a moment before returning to Randolph. "No need to thank me, I suppose we are all family now."

32

Together

A few weeks flew by in a blur of happiness since Willa and I embarked on our journey together. My heart raced every time I was near her. I could not believe my good fortune.

The Magical Bookshop had become our sanctuary, a place where time and space intertwined, allowing us to explore realms beyond imagination. Every day felt like a wondrous adventure, filled with discoveries and shared moments of pure joy.

As we stood side by side in the bookshop, Willa's voice broke through the stillness. "Anne, do you realize that today is Beth's wedding day?" Her eyes sparkled as she grinned at me. My stomach fluttered.

A soft smile tugged at the corners of my lips as I nodded in agreement. "You're right, Willa. We should stop by and offer our congratulations. Beth and Henry deserve all the happiness in the world."

Without hesitation, we made our way to Beth's after-wedding party. The air was alive with laughter and music, the joyful atmosphere contagious. The moment we arrived, Beth's eyes lit up with delight upon seeing us.

"Anne! Willa! I'm so glad you're here." Beth rushed towards us and enveloped us in a warm embrace. "You must meet Henry's half-brother, the real duke."

Edmund, the real Irish duke, was a charming man. He seemed taken with Beth and her adoration of his brother.

As Beth gushed about her love for Henry and the charm of Ireland, my heart lightened. She had gotten everything she wished for. Love had found its way into her life, bringing her the happiness she so deserved.

Willa and I exchanged a glance, her lips quirking into a teasing smile. I exhaled, relaxing my shoulders. We had all found the happiness we deserved. It was strange to think of all the different paths we had taken to find love. I supposed it was a testament to its power.

Willa and I joined the celebration, raising our glasses to toast Beth and Henry's union. I couldn't keep my gaze away from Willa. I was so fortunate to be with her. Pressing myself closer to her, I grasped her hand, the pressure a sweet assurance.

"Ready to depart?" I whispered to Willa.

She nodded, flashing me another one of her infectious smiles.

"Where to?"

She grasped my hand. "Wherever you would like to go."

I had not been to visit my Mama and Mary in a while, so I decided to stop by and look in on my family.

I walked through the familiar threshold of my childhood home, Willa by my side. The sound of our footsteps echoed through the quiet hallways as we made our way to the sitting room. The warmth of nostalgia enveloped me.

As we entered the sitting room, my mama sat in her favorite armchair, engrossed in a book. My brother, Randolph, occupied the adjacent seat, his gaze lost in the flickering flames of the fireplace. They both looked up as we entered, surprise flickering across their faces.

"Anne, dear, Willa, what a pleasant surprise. To what do we owe this visit?" Mama's face brightened at the sight of us.

I smiled. "Mama, I wanted to ask about Mary. Is she here?" My eyes searched the room for any sign of her presence.

Mama's gaze softened. "No, my dear. Mary is out on an outing with Mr. Everton, accompanied by our maid, Elsie."

A delighted surprise coursed through me, my heart quickening its pace. "Mr. Everton? But... he was originally meant to marry me."

Mama's lips curved into a knowing smile. "Yes, dear. It seems that fate had different plans for Mary and Mr. Everton. After the events at the chapel, when you and the others left, Mary and Mr. Everton ended up getting to know one another. He has been visiting often, and their connection has grown."

I couldn't help but feel a surge of happiness for Mary. To witness her find love, and to see her heart bloom after the unexpected turn of events, brought me immeasurable joy. It was as if the universe had realigned itself, steering each of us toward our rightful paths.

"That's wonderful news. Mary deserves all the happiness in the world, and Mr. Everton seems like a fine gentleman."

Randolph, who had been silent until now, spoke up with a nod of agreement. "Indeed, Anne. Mary and Mr. Everton seem to enjoy each other's company. I'm glad they have discovered a connection that brings them joy."

***

As we walked hand in hand, the whisper of the wind playing with our hair, I couldn't help but feel an overwhelming sense of contentment. The worries and uncertainties of the world faded into the background, and all that mattered was the bond between Willa and me.

The location I had chosen for Willa's surprise was a secluded spot nestled amidst a grove of ancient trees. The gentle rays of the setting sun filtered through the leaves, casting a warm golden glow upon the surroundings. It felt as if nature itself had conspired to create the perfect setting for our special moment.

I stopped and turned to face Willa, my heart pounding in my throat. My palms turned slick, and I wiped them on my skirt. With a smile dancing upon my lips, I reached into my pocket, pulling out a small, intricately crafted box. The delicate velvet exterior held within it a token of our love, a symbol of our union.

"Willa, I have something for you." My knees grew weak, and my cheeks burned, but I remained standing. I wanted to give Willa a proper proposal.

Willa's mouth gaped open, her brows raising as she gazed at me. "What's this?" She took a step closer, her eyes fixed on the box in my hand. I sank onto one knee, my leg pressed against the grass. Looking up at her, I smiled.

I opened the box, revealing a delicate silver bracelet adorned with a shimmering garnet in the shape of a heart. The gemstone, in all its red splendor, was a choice I had made to show my love and devotion.

I chewed my lip, holding Willa's gaze. My voice trembled despite my determination to sound smooth. "Willa, this bracelet represents our bond, our connection, and the love that binds us together." My breath hitched. "Willa, will you be my wife?"

Willa's eyes widened, a tinge of red creeping up her freckled cheeks. "Anne...I. Yes. Of course, I will be your wife."

I lifted the bracelet from the box, its silver chain glimmering in the fading light. With a gentle touch, I fastened it around her wrist, feeling the weight of its significance settle upon us both.

"It is beautiful, Anne." I could hear the awe in her voice. "Thank you for this precious gift. I will cherish it always."

Her eyes turned red, and she dropped to her knees in front of me, wrapping her arms around my neck. I buried my nose in the crook of her neck, inhaling her intoxicating scent. "I love you," I whispered in her ear.

Willa pulled back and grabbed my face with both hands, planting her lips against mine, our breaths mingling. I touched my forehead against hers. When we broke apart, I flashed her a smile. "You haven't even read the inscription."

With careful fingers, she turned the bracelet so she could read what I had inscribed on the inside. "Tems Nous Joindra."

Her eyes crinkled, and she grinned. "Time will bring us together."

"I thought it was the perfect inscription to encapsulate what we have been through."

"It is." Willa kissed me again. "I adore it; I adore you."

My heart surged with warmth as I pulled Willa into another embrace, our bodies fitting together in perfect harmony. Whenever I touched her, time stood still.

"You've got my heart and soul. I'm forever bound to you. I love you, Willa."

And as we kneeled in that magical spot, surrounded by nature, our hearts entwined, I knew that this moment would forever be etched in my memory. The journey ahead was filled with infinite possibilities, but in that space, it was just Willa and me, united and ready to face the world together.

Afterword

Thank you for reading *Anne Through Time*. Since writing *Rose Through Time*, the first novel in the A Magical Bookshop Novel series, I wanted to give Anne her own redemption ARc over the course of the series and what better way to do that than to turn the antagonist of the first novel into the heroine of the finale. Whether this is your first time reading one of my time travel novels or if you are a returning reader, I appreciate that you took a chance on my books.

If you have the chance, I would love it if you left a review to share your thoughts about Anne Through Time with other readers on your platform of choice. It would be a tremendous help in getting my story out into the world!

Not yet finished with the world of my A Magical Book-shop Novel series? Continue reading for the first two chapters of the prequel novella *Sage, Rosemary, and Time*. If you'd like to stay up to date on future projects and receive bonus content, sign up for my newsletter on my website!

And as always, happy reading!

Sage, Rosemary, and Time

CHAPTER 1

A Scholarship

"Rosemary, come here," my mother called from the living room, her voice strained yet filled with anticipation. "Look what just arrived."

I dropped the magazine I was reading on top of my bed and rushed down the stairs. As I entered the room, the smell of cigarette smoke mingled with the sound of the television blaring in the background.

A disembodied voice droned from the deep black-and-white television, transposed over footage of soldiers in combat.

"We are only halfway through 1967 and the Vietnam War has already been marked by intense fighting and critical turning points. US forces, alongside South Vietnamese troops, have been engaged in a protracted struggle against the communist Viet Cong and North Vietnamese Army. Let's take a closer look at some of the key developments this year."

My mother sat on the couch, coughing and waving a letter

in the air in one hand while the other held out her preferred brand of cigarette, Virginia Slims.

I glanced out the window and saw the mailman walking away from our front yard, his bag now empty. My heart raced with anticipation. Could it be a response from one of the colleges I had applied to? With an eager step, I approached my mother, nervousness growing in my chest. I had applied to a few; I had never been one to put all my eggs into one basket. But if I had to be honest, there was only one choice for me.

"Is it from the Curtis Institute of Music?"

My mother nodded, taking a final drag from her cigarette before pressing it out in the ashtray on the side table. She reached for the letter opener and slit open the envelope.

The television continued to play.

"Back home, the anti-war movement gains momentum as thousands take to the streets, demanding an end to American involvement in Vietnam."

But my attention was focused on the letter my mother held in her hands. I fidgeted with the buttons on my blouse. "I'm too nervous to read it, Mom. Can you do it for me?"

My mother flashed an understanding smile, a bit of mirth sparkling in her gaze. She turned the TV off, a soft hiss exuding from the screen as it turned black.

"Of course, sweetheart." She licked her fingers and unfolded the neatly pressed letter. Her eyes flitted across the paper, and after clearing her throat, she started to read.

Dear Rosemary Scott,

I am delighted to inform you that you have been selected

as a recipient of a full scholarship at the Curtis Institute of Music for the upcoming academic year.

"I got in?" I became aware that my hands were trembling.

Mother paused, a smile creeping across her face. "Rosemary, you did it. You got accepted." She pushed the letter towards me. "Here, you finish reading it."

I nodded, my heart drumming against my ribcage.

On behalf of the admissions committee and the entire faculty, I extend my warmest congratulations to you.

Your exceptional musical talent and dedication to your craft have truly impressed us. We believe that you possess the potential to make a significant contribution to the world of music, and we are thrilled to offer you this opportunity to further develop your skills and nurture your artistic growth at Curtis.

At the Curtis Institute of Music, you will be joining a prestigious institution renowned for its commitment to excellence in musical education. Our esteemed faculty members are internationally recognized musicians and educators who are dedicated to helping you achieve your highest artistic aspirations. The curriculum at Curtis is designed to provide you with a comprehensive musical education that combines rigorous training, performance opportunities, and a supportive community of fellow musicians.

A surge of exhilaration coursed through my veins, and

I couldn't contain my excitement any longer. I grabbed my mother by the arms, lifting her from the blue pin-tucked couch, and together we jumped.

As we jumped, the front door opened and my brother Lyle walked into the room, a backpack slung across his shoulders, and wearing overalls stained from working at the automotive factory. Confusion clouded his face.

"What's all this about?"

Breathless and beaming, I turned to him. "I got accepted into the Curtis Institute of Music."

Lyle's eyes widened, and a smile tugged at his lips. "Congratulations, Rosemary. I knew you could do it. They would be fools not to accept you."

I dropped my mother's hands and pulled my brother in for a hug, careful not to touch the oily stains on his front. "They gave me a full scholarship."

As my mother caught her breath, a hint of a wheeze still present in her cough, she spoke up, "I'm so proud of you, Rosemary. I never doubted for a moment that you would get in."

"All right, all right, that is enough hugging." Lyle patted my shoulder and peeled my arms away from him. "I am in terrible need of a shower."

I pinched my nose and stuck out my tongue at Lyle. "You do smell."

"Very funny." Lyle shook his head and dropped his backpack next to the coat rack.

Mother chuckled. "How about this; Lyle, you go freshen up while Rosemary heads out to give Mrs. Johnson the good news. Then I can prepare something sweet for after dinner since we are celebrating."

"Fudge cake?" I asked hopefully. It was one of my favorite treats, usually only reserved for birthdays.

Mother glanced at the clock above the TV, lips pursing as she did her calculations. "I should have enough time before dinner is ready."

"Yes, thank you, thank you!" I blew my mom a kiss then snatched my shoes from the entryway, hopping between feet as I pulled them on. "I will be right back."

"Give my thanks to Mrs. Johnson," Mother shouted after me as I hurried out the door.

"Will do, Mom."

I hopped on my bicycle, feeling the hot breeze against my face as I pedaled down the familiar streets of my town. The sunlight streamed through the fanned leaves of the towering palm trees, casting dappled shadows on the pavement below.

As I approached Mrs. Johnson's house, I noticed a fellow student stepping out, the front door still ajar. Mrs. Johnson must have spotted me, for she appeared in the doorway, her eyes twinkling as she crossed her arms.

"Rosemary, my dear, did you forget an appointment?" There was a note of concern in her voice. "I didn't think we had a lesson scheduled for today."

I shook my head, a wide grin spreading across my face. "No, Mrs. Johnson, there's no appointment. I just wanted to stop by and share some incredible news with you."

Her brow raised as I dismounted my bicycle and propped it against the white picket fence. Mrs. Johnson beckoned me inside, and I followed her into the cozy living room, the scent of sweet tea lingering in the air.

"What's this news, my dear?" Mrs. Johnson asked, glancing at me.

I took a deep breath, excitement bubbling in my stomach. "I've been accepted into the Curtis Institute of Music."

Mrs. Johnson's eyes widened, and a gasp escaped her lips. "Rosemary, that's wonderful!" Her voice was filled with pride. "I knew you had it in you, my dear."

Tears shimmered in the corners of my eyes as I looked at the woman who had guided me since I was a little girl through hours of piano practice and hand positions. "I couldn't have done it without you, Mrs. Johnson. Your guidance, patience, and belief in me have been invaluable."

A soft smile graced Mrs. Johnson's face, and she reached out to clasp my hands. "You've always been special, Rosemary." Her gaze turned distant, and her voice filled with warmth. "I remember when you were just ten years old, practicing tirelessly, determined to hit every note. Your dedication has always impressed me."

Memories of long hours spent at the piano flooded my mind, and I felt a surge of gratitude for the lessons and the bond we had shared. Mrs. Johnson had been more than just a teacher; she had become a mentor and a friend. And now, because of her, I would be heading to Philadelphia.

"You're my best student, Rosemary," Mrs. Johnson continued, her voice filled with pride. "And I couldn't be happier that you have this opportunity to use and expand your gift at college."

We sat there for a while, reminiscing about the journey

that had led us to this moment. The afternoon sun cast a warm glow over us, and in the presence of my beloved teacher, I felt a deep sense of determination and gratitude.

As I bid Mrs. Johnson farewell and mounted my bicycle once again, I carried her words with me, a guiding light illuminating my path. With the acceptance letter tucked safely in my pocket, I rode back home, where my mother and brother would be waiting for me.

Soon enough, I sat at the kitchen table, savoring the last few bites of my mother's meatloaf. The comforting aroma filled the air, reminding me of countless family dinners over the years. The taste was familiar and comforting, a testament to my mother's love and care. I sighed, feeling the warmth of the meal spread through my body.

As I wiped my mouth with a napkin, my mother rose from her seat and disappeared into the kitchen. I watched with anticipation as she reappeared, carrying her homemade fudge cake on a floral plate. My eyes lit up, and a smile tugged at the corners of my lips. Fudge cake was my absolute favorite.

Placing the cake in the center of the table, my mother grabbed a knife and began to slice it, each piece landing on a waiting plate with precision. My older brother, Lyle, shifted in his seat beside me, his eyes fixed on the mouthwatering dessert.

With the plates of fudge cake now in front of us, we each took a forkful and savored the rich, velvety sweetness. The chocolate melted on my tongue, a decadent indulgence that made my taste buds dance with delight.

Around me, the sound of my family's contented murmurs filled the kitchen. Lyle grinned, licking the last of the frosting from his fork, and my mother's eyes twinkled with affection. At that moment, I couldn't help but feel an overwhelming sense of happiness, a warmth that enveloped me from within.

A deep appreciation swelled in my heart as I glanced at my family. Here they were, supporting me in all my dreams and aspirations. They had been there for every recital, every late-night practice session, and every setback I had encountered along the way ever since father passed away when I was five.

I took another bite of the fudge cake. The future lay ahead, full of promise and possibilities. The acceptance into the Curtis Institute of Music was just the beginning, the stepping stone to a world of melodies and harmonies waiting to be explored.

I couldn't imagine being happier.

As I savored the last crumbs of the fudge cake, I held onto this moment, etching it into the deepest recesses of my heart.

With a soft smile, I whispered to myself, "This is happiness."

CHAPTER 2

An Errand

The next day, as the sun cast its golden rays across our small town, the mailman arrived once again, carrying news that wouldn't bring the same joy as the previous day. My heart sank as I watched Lyle's hands tremble, his grip tight on the envelope he clutched. The distinctive emblem of the Selective Service System stamped on it felt like a heavy weight on the otherwise thin letter.

Lyle's voice quivered as he spoke, his words laced with fear and resignation. "Rosemary, I've been selected to report for a physical examination." His voice wavered, and he cleared his throat. We all knew what receiving a draft notice meant. Many men from our town, our neighbors, and our friends, had already been selected and sent to fight overseas.

I reached out, placing a comforting hand on his shoulder. "Maybe there's still a chance they'll disqualify you." I tried to infuse hope into my words. "They can't take everyone."

Lyle's response was laced with a bitter truth. "I'm of good, healthy, American stock, Rosemary." His voice was tinged with sadness. "There's nothing physically wrong with me. Look at how many men from our town have already been called away to fight. I doubt they'll pass me over."

His words hung in the air, heavy with the reality of the situation. The draft had cast its net far and wide, and now it had ensnared my brother, threatening to tear him away from the life he knew. The weight of the situation settled upon us like a suffocating fog.

***

A few weeks passed, and the days blurred together as our town bid farewell to more of its young men, sending them off to unknown fates. Lyle, too, prepared himself for the inevitable. He packed his belongings, his steps heavy.

As he stood by the bus stop, ready to ride out and begin his basic training, I stood beside him, my eyes brimming with tears that threatened to spill over. We exchanged a solemn gaze, a silent understanding passing between us.

Time stood still; the world hushed as we confronted the reality of war. With a heavy heart, I watched him drive off into the distance, the bus becoming smaller and smaller until it blended with the horizon. As he disappeared, I whispered a prayer for his safety, for his return.

Panic gripped my heart when I returned home and found my mother slumped over on the kitchen floor, her fragile form trembling. Tears streaked her cheeks, and her labored breaths echoed through the room. Fear coursed through my veins, urging me into action.

Kneeling beside her, I cradled her in my arms, my voice trembling with desperation. "Mom, please, stay calm. I need to go get help. Just hold on, okay?"

Her eyes met mine, and she nodded weakly, struggling to catch her breath. I rose to my feet, my heart pounding against my chest. We did not yet have a phone at home, and time was of the essence. I had to find someone who could call for an ambulance.

With hurried steps, I rushed out of the house, my mind racing. I ran towards our neighbor's home, my fists pounding on their front door. I could hear my voice, frantic and filled with urgency, calling out for help.

The door swung open, revealing Mrs. Thompson, her face etched with concern as she took in my flustered state. "Rosemary, dear, what's happened?"

Struggling to catch my breath, I blurted out the words, my voice trembling with fear. "I need to call an ambulance. It's my mother. She's... she's in trouble."

Mrs. Thompson's eyes widened, and without hesitation, she ushered me inside. Her living room blurred before my eyes as she rushed to pick up the phone, dialing the emergency number. I could hear her voice, steady and composed, as she relayed the details to the operator.

I stood there, feeling a mix of helplessness and gratitude. Mrs. Thompson had always been kind, but at that moment, her compassion and willingness to assist overwhelmed me.

As Mrs. Thompson hung up the phone, she turned to me, her voice gentle yet firm. "Help is on the way, Rosemary." She rested her hand on my shoulder. "Stay strong, my dear. Your mother will be taken care of."

Together, we waited, each passing second feeling like an eternity. As the distant wail of sirens grew louder, a surge of hope washed over me. Help was coming, and though the future remained uncertain, I clung to the belief that my mother would receive the care she needed. That she would be all right.

And as the ambulance arrived, its flashing lights illuminating the darkening sky, I whispered a silent prayer to whoever was out there listening.

My heart felt heavy as I sat beside my mother in the ambulance, the rhythmic hum of the vehicle punctuating the tense silence. Fear and uncertainty hung in the air, suffocating me as we embarked on this daunting journey.

Minutes later, we arrived at the hospital, and a whirlwind of activity surrounded us. Medical professionals whisked my mother away, promising to take good care of her. I clung to those words, seeking solace in the hope they offered.

Hours dragged by, each passing minute amplifying my anxiety. Finally, the doctor returned to my mother's hospital room, a solemn expression etched on his face. I held my breath, my hands clasped in my lap, awaiting his words.

He pulled up a chair, his eyes filled with empathy, and began to speak. "I've reviewed the x-ray images, and I'm afraid the results are not what we had hoped for." His voice was gentle but tinged with sadness. "Your mother has stage three lung cancer."

The room spun around me as his words settled in. Cancer. The mere mention of the word sent a chill down my spine, filling me with terror and despair. I glanced at my mother, her face pale, her eyes reflecting the shock that mirrored my own.

The doctor continued, explaining the treatment plan that lay ahead. "We will need to start chemotherapy immediately. It's a challenging road, but with the right treatment, there is hope."

Tears welled up in my eyes as I listened, my mind struggling to comprehend the magnitude of what lay before us. I reached out, grasping my mother's hand, offering whatever comfort I could though my mind overflowed with troubling thoughts.

How could it be that only two weeks ago my life had been the happiest it could ever be? Newly graduated from high school, accepted into the Curtis Institute of Music on a full scholarship, and my family together and happily celebrating my achievements. Now, my brother was off to fight in Vietnam. I hadn't been able to listen to the news since, not when it was filled with reports of attacks and men killed. My heart sank. And my mother was ill.

There would be no more going to Philadelphia. I could not leave my mother to deal with doctor visits and chemo treatment by herself. She was going to need me. I felt my dreams of becoming a renowned pianist slipping through my fingers.

Gathering my courage, I turned to the doctor, my voice trembling but resolute. "Thank you for your honesty and for outlining the treatment plan." I grasped my mother's pale hand. "We will fight this together."

The doctor nodded, his gaze filled with compassion. "You're both strong, and with the support of our medical team, we'll do everything we can to help."

As the doctor left the room, leaving us with the weight of our new reality, I squeezed my mother's hand, vowing to be her pillar of strength. "We'll fight this, Mom. I'll be right by your side every step of the way."

"What about school? You're supposed to leave in a month."

I worried my lip as I gazed at my mother's concerned face. "I can postpone a year; I am certain they'll let me." I knew it was a lie when I said it. The Curtis Institute of Music was highly competitive, and there were very few slots available each year, let alone applicants who received full scholarships. If I did not go now, I might never go. But my mother did not need to know that.

"Sweetheart, I don't want to come in between your dreams."

I brushed the side of my mom's face with my hand, her skin clammy to the touch. "You aren't. I promise."

***

Once my mother was discharged, our life changed drastically. Responsibility was pressed upon my shoulders as I balanced the demands of caring for my mother and the necessity of keeping our household afloat. It had been a few weeks since her diagnosis, and life had become a delicate dance of tending to her needs while juggling the burdens of everyday life.

Cooking, cleaning, and running errands had become my daily routine. But in the face of mounting hospital bills, I knew I needed to do more. That's why I had taken up a job at the local diner, named Grace's Place, to ensure that we could continue to make ends meet.

Amid my hectic schedule, I found myself at the town's pharmacy, standing in line to fill one of my mother's prescriptions. The familiar scent of medicine filled the air, mingling with the sound of customers murmuring their own stories of health and healing.

Finally, it was my turn. I approached the counter, clutching the prescription in my hands. The pharmacist, a kind-eyed man named Mr. Jenkins, greeted me with a warm smile.

"Hello, dear. I see you're here to pick up your mother's medication."

I nodded, offering a small smile in return. "Yes, it's an anti-nausea medication. She's been having a tough time with the side effects of the treatment."

Mr. Jenkins reached for the prescription and began processing it. As he typed away on the computer, I couldn't help but feel a glimmer of hope that this medication would bring some relief to my mother, even if just a little.

After a few moments, Mr. Jenkins turned to me, his expression apologetic. "I'm afraid we're currently running low on stock for that medication. It will only be a little while before we can fill it. Would you mind running a few errands and coming back later?"

A pang of disappointment tugged at my heart, but I understood that sometimes these things were beyond our control. "Of course, Mr. Jenkins. I'll run a few errands and be back as soon as I can."

With a grateful nod, I left the pharmacy, my mind already shifting gears, mapping out things I could do to pass the time since it made no sense to return home in the meantime.

As I snapped out of my thoughts, my gaze wandered up and landed on a peculiar sight. A bookshop, nestled among the row of buildings, stood before me, its antiquated appearance contrasting with the modern surroundings.

How had I never noticed it before?

Intrigue swelled within me, a magnetic pull drawing me toward the mysterious shop. Curiosity danced in my eyes as I stepped across the threshold, the door's bell tinkling, announcing my arrival. The air inside was heavy with the scent of old books, a fragrance that enveloped me like a comforting embrace.

The bookshelves, reaching towards the ceiling, held volumes upon volumes of literary treasures. Dust particles floated in the warm glow of the dim lighting. I felt a sense of wonder and nostalgia, as though stepping into a different era altogether.

There, amidst the rows of books, a particular shelf caught my attention. It beckoned me closer, whispering secrets only I could hear. Following the invisible thread of curiosity, I traced my fingers along the spines until I found myself inexplicably drawn to a small, green book without a title. Its worn cover held an air of mystery as if it held within its pages something extraordinary.

Without hesitating, I plucked the book from its resting place, cradling it in my hands. As I opened it, a surge of anticipation coursed through my veins. But as soon as the pages touched my fingertips, a strange sensation rippled through me. It was as though the world around me compressed, folding in on itself.

Suddenly, everything went dark. The book slipped from my grasp, disappearing into the void. Panic gripped my heart as I realized I, too, had vanished.

Acknowledgments

If you've made it this far, I want to give a big thank you to everyone who has helped me publish this book. I am incredibly grateful for the kind and enthusiastic responses to my novels, something that far exceeds anything I could have imagined when I started publishing. It truly warms my heart and brightens my spirits when the writing gets tough.

With the finale to my A Magical Bookshop Novel series done and in the hands of readers, I'm ready to continue writing new stories in different genres. I hope to continue to entertain and enchant in new worlds and with new characters but there may always be another small return to my A Magical Bookshop Novel series in the form of short stories. Do you have any characters you would love to read a short story about? Tag me on social media or shoot me an email and who knows... Perhaps your favorite character will pop up again as the hero or heroine of their own short story.

I hope you'll continue reading my future novels.

I also want to give a shoutout to my editor, Megan Sanders, who has been along for the ride since my first novel, Rose Through Time, back in 2021. And Patterson Photography for my beautiful author photos. Last but not least, I want to thank you for reading because without you I wouldn't be doing what I love.

May we meet again in the next book!

About The Author

Harmke Buursma is a writer, and author of the book Rose Through Time. She uses her background in Journalism to help bring her fictional characters and worlds to life. When she isn't writing, she likes to read as many books as she can get her hands on. Originally born and raised in The Netherlands, Harmke now lives in Las Vegas with her husband Matthew and two dogs.

For more information about Harmke and her books, visit www.harmkebuursma.com.

Harmke Buursma
Photo by Patterson Photography

Books by this Author

ROSE THROUGH TIME

WILLIAM THROUGH TIME

BETH THROUGH TIME

ANNE THROUGH TIME

SAGE, ROSEMARY, AND TIME

Audiobooks

Rose Through Time now also available as an audiobook narrated by Krista Nicely

Rediscover the magic of the first installment of the A Magical Bookshop Novel series now available on Amazon, Audible, and Itunes.

For more information, check out
www.harmkebuursma.com